Ten feet separated them.

Carter made it in two steps. At the same time, he tensed the forearm muscle in his right arm. Hugo's hilt was warm in his palm as his left arm encircled the guard's throat.

The stiletto came up, under Carter's left arm and into the man's neck. Death was instantaneous, but before the Killmaster could withdraw the blade, Georgette was gasping a warning.

NICK CARTER IS IT!

FROM THE NICK CARTER
KILLMASTER SERIES

NICK CARTER

KILLMASTER

The Cyclops Conspiracy

CHARTER BOOKS, NEW YORK

THE CYCLOPS CONSPIRACY

A Charter Book/published by arrangement with
The Condé Nast Publications, Inc.

PRINTING HISTORY
Charter edition/May 1986

ISBN: 0-441-57282-0

Charter Books are published by The Berkley Publishing Group,
200 Madison Avenue, New York, New York 10016.
PRINTED IN THE UNITED STATES OF AMERICA

*Dedicated to the men of the
Secret Services of the United
States of America*

ONE

As it had every Sunday for the last two months, the phone call came at exactly nine in the morning.

"Romar?"

"Yes, Mulata."

"He is gone . . . golf until five this evening." The phone went dead in Romar de Armon's ear.

It was a code they had. Jorge Bondawa would be playing golf all that afternoon. The servants would be off, away from the Clichy château. It meant a summons from Bondawa's aging but still beautiful—and quite bored—wife, Mulata.

De Armon, as he did every Sunday morning, called Air France and made a reservation on the Concorde for Dulles Airport in the United States. Hopefully, this Sunday he would be able to use that reservation.

Each time he had made that call his hands shook, as they did now. It was a dangerous game he played. He had been hired by a private party to get the documents. But De Armon was greedy. He reasoned that if the documents were so valuable to a private party, how much more valuable would they be to a government . . . *any* government?

He had put out bids, and the United States had won.

He loaded his coat pockets with his passport, cash, and the

1

tiny camera they had given him. A prepacked bag was already in his car. It had been there, ready, for eight weeks.

In his aging Fiat he drove north out of Paris to the wealthy residential area of Clichy. Two blocks from the residence of Togo's ambassador to France, he parked and walked the rest of the way.

As usual, Mulata Bondawa met him at the door only partially clothed. In this case, it was a pair of diaphanous panties and a blouse with no bra beneath it. She swayed a little as she kissed him. She had obviously already been drinking heavily that morning.

They had their obligatory drink in the sitting room just off the bedroom. This lasted, as usual, for five minutes. Then the tall, statuesque woman stood.

"Let's go into the bedroom."

She dropped her panties to the floor, leaving only the blouse to cover the upper part of her full-figured body. As she walked toward the bedroom, her backside jiggled delightfully in tempo with her graceful strides.

Even though she was more than twenty years Romar de Armon's senior, and he had much stronger reasons than sex to be in the house, the sight of her aroused him. That was why they had chosen him to insinuate himself with this woman and seduce her.

Romar de Armon loved all women. And because of his exotic handsomeness and magnificent physique, there were few women who didn't fall under his spell.

Outside, de Armon heard a low rumble. It stopped him in his tracks. At the doorway, she paused and looked back at him still standing in the center of the room.

"What's wrong?"

"That's thunder."

"So what?"

"Thunder means rain. You can't play golf in the rain."

She shrugged and beckoned him with a long-nailed finger. There was not the slightest bit of request in her manner now.

It was total and complete command.

He followed her, and felt the blood pounding in his groin as she stretched her nearly naked body across the bed.

"Come and make love to me, Romar, darling," she crooned, raising her arms to him.

As he stripped, his mind was mesmerized by the erotic display in front of him.

Outside, another low roll of thunder.

"Jesus, Mulata . . ."

"Hurry, Romar, hurry," she moaned, caressing herself.

With a rumble in his throat not unlike the thunder outside, Romar de Armon fell between her lush thighs.

He stood, looking down at her sleeping form on the bed. With all the makeup rubbed off and her hair tousled in disarray, Mulata looked every one of her years.

But her years hadn't diminished her carnal desires, nor her capacity for alcohol. For over two hours they had made violent love, and drank more drinks than he could remember before she had given up at last and passed out.

Dressed, he walked back down to the château's main floor. In the study he went directly to the large portrait of Togo's president, Jacques Goulanda, and moved it aside. He had no need to check the combination of the safe behind the portrait. By now he knew it by heart.

Seconds later the contents of the safe were spread before him on the desk. Quickly he rifled through them, then suddenly stopped.

It was there, the secret agreement, signed and witnessed.

De Armon's hands shook as he spread the many pages of the document out and photographed each one. Every time the shutter clicked, his nerves jumped. But they were quickly calmed by his brain.

All he could see were American dollar signs, a quarter of a million of them.

When he was finished he carefully put the pages back

together and replaced everything in the safe. Pocketing the camera, he scurried to the door and let himself out.

The rain had started. Halfway to his car he saw the black Citroën with the two flags on the front fenders.

Romar de Armon averted his face when the silver-haired black man in the back seat of the car looked his way.

My God, he thought, *I just made it!*

The man in the rear of the sedan was Jorge Bondawa.

At a gas station just before the Orly Airport exit, De Armon turned off and parked near a phone booth.

The number answered on the first ring. "Yes?"

"The moon is bright over Capri."

"*Bonjour, mon ami*. How did we fare today?"

"Nothing, I'm afraid. In fact there was nothing new in the safe at all."

The man on the other end of the line sighed. "That's too bad. Our people in Togo tell me that their agreement seems close to consummation. You examined every document in the safe?"

"Every one, carefully. Nothing."

"Very well. Let us hope next Sunday bears sweeter fruit. Until then, de Armon. *Au revoir*."

"*Oui, monsieur*."

De Armon drove on to Orly. He parked in the short-term parking lot, extracted his bag from the trunk, and bid good-bye forever to the dented Fiat. Inside the terminal he confirmed his ticket, paid for it in cash, and presented his passport.

"Boarding in a half hour, monsieur."

"*Merci*."

He bypassed the boarding area for the moment and went directly to the international telephone exchange. He jotted down the memorized number the American agent had given him and passed it to the girl along with a long-distance overseas deposit.

It took five minutes to raise an overseas operator. From there the call went through quickly.

"Your number is ringing, monsieur. Booth three."

"*Merci.*"

He stepped into the booth, picked up the receiver, and waited until he heard the operator's key click out before he spoke.

"This is Romar."

"One moment."

In less than that, the woman's voice was replaced by a male growl. "Yes, this is Contact Blue. Go ahead."

De Armon sighed in relief. It was all going the way the agent in Paris said it would.

"I have the information, all of it, on film. I will be in the United States by tonight."

"Very well."

"Have you made arrangements for authentication of the documents, and authorization of the money?"

"We have."

"Excellent. Tomorrow night, at ten o'clock sharp, I will meet you in the lounge of the Bay Motel in Riviera Beach, Maryland."

"We know the place. The same man who contacted you in Paris will make the meet and take you to the proper people."

"Carter?"

"Yes. We felt it would be easier that way, since you can recognize him."

"Very good," de Armon replied.

He hung up and walked by the exchange operator without getting his receipt or his change on the call.

Who needed small change? he mused. In two days he would be worth $250,000.

An extraordinarily tall man with huge shoulders and over-size hands stood at the rail of the Concorde boarding area, watching every move Romar de Armon made. His big jaw chewed casually on a whole package of gum, and his thick fingers idly flicked nonexistent ash from the end of an unlit cigar.

He waited until all the passengers, including De Armon, had gone through the door and down the walkway to the needlelike plane before turning away.

It was only a few steps to a pay phone, where he dialed a number from memory.

"Oui?"

"Monsieur Cologne, si'l vous plaît."

"Oui."

He dropped the gum from the end of his tongue into a trash receptacle and jammed the cigar between his teeth.

"Cologne here."

"It's Bowldor, monsieur. I picked him up at the Bondawa house in Clichy."

"Yes?"

"He did not return to his own flat today. He drove toward Orly, and stopped to make a call from a gas station."

"That was probably when he called me. Go on."

"He went on to an Orly parking lot, left his car, and picked up a ticket."

"Damn! He's got it and he's selling us out!"

"He made an overseas call before he boarded. You said not to scare him, so I let him go."

"You did well, Bowldor. I have already planned for an eventuality such as this. The man has the face and body of Adonis, but I'm afraid he has the greed of Midas. What flight?"

"The Concorde to Dulles."

"Very well, I shall turn it over to New York."

"Oui, monsieur."

Bowldor hung up and walked toward the main terminal exit. Halfway there he paused, deep in thought, and made a detour toward the overseas exchange.

It was empty.

"Mademoiselle?"

"*Oui*?"

"I am a private investigator working with Interpol." He flashed the open wallet across her eyes so fast that she hardly saw its contents, then he described De Armon and told her what he wanted.

"But, monsieur, that is against the rules. My supervisor would—"

". . . never know about it," he replied, smoothing a one-thousand-franc note on the blotter before her. "We working people must stay together, don't you agree?"

The girl eyed his smile and the bill. She moved her pad over the money and flipped her record sheet twice. Quickly she scribbled down the Washington, D.C., number, tore off the sheet, and pushed it across the desk.

"Anything to help the police, monsieur," she said with a tight smile.

"Of course, mademoiselle. *Merci*."

He pocketed the number and strolled away.

Cyclops International was a huge international conglomerate with many fingers reaching into many places.

It wouldn't be too hard to trace the number.

She ran her fingers through her blond hair, cut short like a helmet to her head, and leaned close to the mirror. She rubbed the sleep from her eyes and pinched her cheeks to make them rosy.

"Good morning, Marga," she said to the face in the mirror. "You're as elfin and sweetly innocent as ever."

She smiled and examined her profile, first from the left and then from the right. She had a nice smile and nice teeth.

Moving from the dressing room into the bath, she set the tub's taps to gushing. Outside, ringing clearly over the running water, she could hear the bells of nearby St. Patrick's calling the faithful to seven o'clock mass.

"Hail Mary, full of grace," she chanted, returning to the

dressing room and the mirror. "Forgive me, Father, for I
have sinned . . ." She smoothed the satin lapel of the
dressing gown against her cheek, then shrugged it from her
shoulders. "But without sin, how can a girl get ahead in this
world?"

She studied her nude body in the glass. She was in good
shape. Her shoulders were set squarely, her breasts were
small but well formed, her belly was flat, her hips and
buttocks were boyish, and her legs were tapered nicely from
thighs to delicate feet.

She struck several modeling poses, and flashed her innocent yet seductive smile at the mirror over her shoulder. Then
she stood full front, running her hands over her body and
pausing to push up her breasts and to pout at their smallness.

But the pout quickly dissolved into another smile.

Her small breasts, like her boyish body and childlike face,
were all part of her stock in trade, her image of sweet
innocence.

It was that image that had allowed her, through the years,
to get close enough to her prey and disarm them mentally.

Her name was Marga Lund. She was thirty-two years old,
appeared to be in her early twenties, and since the age of
fifteen had personally killed twelve people.

Marga was orphaned at the age of eight, when her father
had beat her mother to death in a drunken rage and then killed
himself in sober remorse.

At twelve she had run away from the state home in Düssel-
dorf and drifted into petty crime. Minor crimes, ranging from
prostitution to larceny, grew into a major crime when she
murdered a man she was blackmailing. She was acquitted of
the murder charge because of her age and a plea of self-
defense. But she did serve a brief sentence for blackmail.

During that incarceration she was recruited by a radical
left-wing group. On her release she had taken part in several
robberies and several bombings all over Germany.

None of this was in the pursuit of any cause. It was, for
Marga, the pursuit of profit.

After claiming her second victim she was very nearly caught, but through the terrorist underground she escaped to Italy and eventually to North Africa. There she became involved in the Communist party and was sent to the Kosikov terrorist school outside Moscow.

She had excelled.

But once again, terrorism and causes didn't interest Marga. The training it provided, however, did. Once she got that, she abandoned her sponsors and struck out on a very profitable career of free-lance killing.

That is, until she was brought to the attention of Marcus Cologne. He saw in Marga even more potential, and groomed her to exploit it.

She shut off the taps and was about to submerge herself in the tub, when the dressing room phone sounded. She had two phone lines in her Fifth Avenue apartment. The dressing room phone was the very private line.

Only one person had the number.

"Good morning, Marcus."

"Good morning, my dear. Splendid, you're awake."

"It's Sunday morning, Marcus. You know I always attend ten o'clock mass."

"Yes, of course. But I fear your absolutions will have to be put off this morning."

"Oh?"

"It's happened."

"Romar de Armon?"

"Yes. We believe he has photographs of the agreement and has decided to strike out on his own."

"Foolish man."

"Very. He boarded the Concorde at Orly a few moments ago."

"New York or Washington?"

"Dulles. Can you leave at once?"

"Of course."

"You have the photograph I sent you?"

Marga slid open a drawer of the dressing table. Inside was

the photo of a very tall, very well built, immaculately dressed man descending a long flight of stairs with a woman on each arm.

"A very attractive man."

"Very, but cunning if cornered. Watch yourself."

"Marcus . . ."

"I know, my dear. You have never failed. Be sure he has the film before disposing of him. And also . . ."

"Yes?"

"Try to get a line on who he was going to sell to."

"I will. See you soon, Marcus."

"Very well, my dear."

Marga hung up and slid the top photo aside. Beneath it was a second picture, a blowup of the face.

She felt a ripple go up her spine as she scanned the rather weak, dimpled chin, the slightly too-sensual lips, and the aquiline, wide-nostriled nose.

Only when she looked at the eyes did she feel any warning or respect for the man.

They were hooded, a deep, almost chocolate brown, and they were cold. Even in the photograph they registered no feeling or recognition of the world they looked upon.

"He has the eyes," she whispered, "the eyes of a predator. It should be a challenging game."

Her own eyes drifted back up to the mirror. Her body shook with an almost sexual tremor.

"Romar de Armon . . . number thirteen."

Gently, she pressed her lips to the matched pair in the mirror.

With a powerful kicking motion of his long legs, Nick Carter urged his body through the water, forcing it to perform at its peak. In and around the simulated coral he glided, daring the jagged edges to rip at his back and legs.

He spotted the escape hatch. Only twenty-five more yards, but all of it straight down.

And then it happened, twenty feet down when he was nearly out of air. From the tangled, waving flora beneath him came a large blue fish. It was moving so fast he was sure it was a fish.

But fish don't have flippers.

The arm came up in a wide arc, the blue-gloved hand extended by a thin-bladed stiletto. He saw the glint of light on steel just in time to tuck and roll aside.

Carter made a lot of target, hard to miss completely. He felt the blade along the muscle of his left shoulder, and then the burn as salt invaded the scratch.

The other man was one hell of a powerful swimmer. He shot by Carter as if he were motorized. Just below the surface, the blurry figure did a backflip, a roll, and hovered between Carter and air.

Carter's lungs were bursting. Through slitted eyes he scanned the situation and knew there was no way around, only through. He rolled to his back and scissor-kicked a few yards. The blue blur moved inch for inch with him, hovering, the stiletto poised.

As Carter moved, he narrowed the depth between them. Then it was only a matter of feet. It was like a well-choreographed water ballet as the deadly arm arched up and Carter drew his legs up until the knees found his chest.

Then straight up, like two uncoiled springs, went the feet directly into the man's gut.

Carter passed him so close their bodies touched. Then he was striking out, breathing only when necessary, keeping his face in the water, his eyes searching.

Stretched out, swimming on the surface, he made a beautiful target. But at least, he thought, speed would be in his favor.

He was wrong.

Against the purples and blues on the bottom, the rubber-clad swimmer was even harder to distinguish. But Carter spotted the bubbles from the lightweight, short tanks. They were keeping up with him easily.

This time he didn't wait to defend. He went on the attack. Rolling forward and kicking up, he knifed like a thick arrow, straight down.

Again the stiletto, in both hands this time, came up, heading for his belly. But the twisting body was out of sync with the arms. Carter grabbed the wrists and rolled his butt under until he felt smooth rubber between his thighs. He locked them around the midsection, caught his feet, and squeezed. At the same time, he twisted the wrists in his powerful grip.

The man was fair-sized but no match for Carter's bulk and brute strength. The fingers released the stiletto, and even though Carter couldn't see them, he knew the eyes behind the dark-tinted mask were growing wider and wider as air was squeezed from the body by the vise of the Killmaster's legs.

"Enough, N3, you've got him! Don't kill him—the match is yours!"

The voice came from a minuscule receiver behind Carter's left ear.

He released the man in the rubber suit and kicked to the surface. Seconds later he crawled from the tank and accepted a towel from Dr. Robert Ross, head of CIA and AXE special training.

"Your reflexes are still excellent, N3, but the body is slowing down a little," the doctor sighed.

"No kidding."

"You should have reached the hatch before you spotted him," Ross continued. "As it was, you had no choice but to fight."

Carter smiled. "But I won."

"Yeah, you won," the other man admitted, returning the grin. "You're good for another year."

The doctor scrawled his signature across Carter's physical report and handed it over.

"See you, Ross," Carter said, moving to the showers.

"Yeah, Nick. Stay alive."

He was just peeling out of his wet suit when a young navy ensign in uniform bustled up to him.

"Mr. Carter?"

"Yeah?"

"Call from Langley, sir. A Mr. Sievers with State. You can take it in the equipment room office, right over there."

"Thanks."

Carter wrapped a towel around his middle and moved into the office. Bob Sievers was liaison between the State Department and the CIA at Langley. As AXE's top Killmaster, Carter rarely had anything to do with either department, but lately, because he had been on the scene, Carter had helped them out on a couple of simple jobs.

"Bob, Nick Carter."

"Hi, Nick, how did it go? They said you were in the tank."

"Fine. I'm cleared to be shot at for another year. What's up?"

"Nothing big, just a little favor. Remember a connection you made for us in Paris a month or so ago? A guy by the name of Romar de Armon?"

Carter squinted his eyes in concentration. A millisecond later the dark, too-handsome face swam up from his subconscious.

"He wanted to sell proof of a KGB-backed coup in some West African country, right?"

"Right . . . Togo."

"Got it," Carter said. "At the time, you thought it might be phony but couldn't chance passing it up, so I made the offer."

"That's it. Turns out that our boy might have the goods. He wants a meet tomorrow night down in Maryland. I'd like to send you if it's no problem. Since he's already seen you, he'll probably feel safe."

"You're clipping my wings, Roberto. I've been trying to

get close to a redhead in the SEC offices named Yvonne for two weeks. Tomorrow night was supposed to be the night.''

"No problem. Take her along. It will make an even better cover. It's all expenses paid on the bay for a couple of days. Who's her chief?''

"Riley.''

"I'll clear some time off for her. Deal?''

"You're on. We'll leave tonight.''

"Good enough. It's the Bay Hotel in Riviera Beach. The meet's for ten sharp in the lounge. Can you stop by here for a quick briefing? You'll be taking him to an authenticator and a pay officer.''

"Sure, an hour.''

"Fine, see you then.''

Carter depressed the phone button, let it go, and dialed a Georgetown number. It rang several times, and he was about to hang up, when a soft voice breathed, "Hello?''

"Yvonne, Nick Carter.''

"Hi. Sorry I took so long. I was in the shower.'' She laughed. "I'm dripping all over the rug.''

Carter smiled, visualizing all that body naked and dripping.

Yvonne Molina was tall and voluptuous, with legs that moved under a dress like scissors clicking. She had green eyes that smoked, and a classic Mediterranean face. In five years she would be fat, but right now she was exotically beautiful.

"I'll let you get back to your shower. How would you like a couple of days down on the bay?''

"With you? . . . I'd love it! But when?''

"I'll pick you up in a couple of hours.''

"No can do. I have to work tomorrow.''

"No, you don't. I have clout,'' he said with a chuckle.

Her laugh was like little brass bells tinkling in his ear. "I'll be packed.''

"*Ciao.*''

Carter whistled as he returned to his locker.

A perfect deal, he thought, and easy. All he had to do was pilot de Armon to his loot, oversee the exchange of goods, and then it was back to delicious Yvonne.

The business did have some compensations after all.

TWO

Romar de Armon was ambitious and devious, but he wasn't too cunning. He didn't know who had hired him to seduce Mulata Bondawa and steal the agreement between representatives of the USSR and General Izak Tebessa of Togo.

He guessed that it wasn't some government, and that had proved correct when he contacted the American embassy in Paris. They had sent an American agent to meet him at once.

From that, he reasoned that his employer, who had hired him for the pittance of ten thousand dollars, was some private individual.

Had Romar de Armon guessed the far-reaching power and the magnitude of his employer, he would never have engineered his escape in such a slipshod manner.

He would not have gone directly to the airport, nor would he have used his own identification to leave the country and rent a car at Dulles International Airport.

But then, De Armon was basically not a criminal. He didn't think like a criminal. He also had a colossal ego.

As he pulled off the Washington Beltway toward Baltimore, the last thought in his head was that someone might be following him.

He passed a couple of slow-moving trucks and came up on a little gray Jaguar convertible doddering along at the legal speed.

The top was down, revealing a blond woman with a very pretty profile. She had a white scarf tied around her head, with its tail trailing behind her.

De Armon pulled abreast of her but didn't pass immediately.

The woman's head turned. Wraparound sunglasses obscured her eyes. Suddenly she smiled. De Armon smiled back and gave her a quick salute of his right hand, which she returned.

Should he bother? Romar mused. Should he take the time?

Suddenly he chuckled aloud. Soon he would have all the time and all the money in the world. He would also have all the women he wanted.

No, now was not the time.

He jammed the accelerator, and the rental car shot forward around the little sports car.

De Armon passed by the Bay Motel and cruised on down the narrow avenue to another bayside hotel called the Yankee Clipper. It was his single homage to security, not staying in the same motel as the one where the meeting with the American agent, Carter, would take place.

The lushness of the streetside foliage gave way to a huge, ugly parking lot and then the hotel entrance. Two young, garishly uniformed men attacked the car. De Armon surrendered the keys and his suitcase, but he carried the briefcase himself.

The lobby was modern gauche, with polished terrazzo floors and two smoked-glass elevators whispering silently between floors. The elevators sported twinkling colored lights on their bottoms.

"Yes, sir?"

"I don't have a reservation . . ."

"No problem, sir. Would you prefer a room in the main building or a bungalow?"

De Armon glanced down at the floor plan of the hotel and the grounds. He remembered the cute little blonde taking the bay turnoff out of Baltimore behind him.

There might be a chance, a pleasant coincidence. . . .

"A room, please . . . in the front."

In the room, he opened the briefcase and removed the four cans of film. Only two of the cans were exposed. He deposited the film in the hollow behind the masking at the top of the drapes and returned to the briefcase. From it he produced a bottle of Cointreau and poured himself a drink.

It was half finished when he saw the Jaguar pull into the drive.

De Armon opened the window's outer shutter, rested his elbows on the sill, and leaned out far enough to hear.

"Will you be staying with us, ma'am?"

"No, I'm just stopping for dinner."

The parking valet roared through the lot in the Jaguar, and the woman entered the hotel.

What luck! De Armon thought, gulping the rest of the drink.

Quickly he stripped, showered, and shaved. He doused his neck and shoulders liberally with cologne, and dressed in an off-white shirt, black trousers with a razor crease, and a blue blazer.

"Dashing, if I do say so myself," he said with a grin to his image in the mirror, then headed for the dining room.

Marga sat alone in a far corner of the dining room. Throughout the meal she had glanced up only a few times to meet his eyes. When he ordered brandy and coffee, she did the same.

He had smiled at her several times, but Marga had kept a mask of cool impassiveness on her face. Only when she rose to leave did she return his smile.

She paid the check and walked into the lobby.

"Your car, ma'am?"

"Not quite yet. I think I'll walk down and look at the bay."

"Of course. It's a lovely evening."

The rear of the hotel was occupied by a horseshoe of bungalows, smooth green lawns, and a huge swimming pool. Steam rose from the heated water and evaporated in the cool night air. The whole was lighted by a few hundred skillfully concealed bulbs.

What an idyllic place to relax, she thought. Or die.

She was through the trees and halfway down the slope toward the bay, when she heard his step on the graveled path behind her.

"Excuse me . . ."

"What? . . . Oh, you frightened me!"

"Sorry. I saw you on the highway out of Washington."

"Oh?" She smiled, revealing even white teeth. "I don't remember."

"I think you do."

She shrugged and laughed. "Perhaps I do."

"May I buy you an after-dinner drink in the lounge?"

"I don't think so. I live nearby, and I have a very jealous husband."

It was De Armon's turn to laugh. "Then may I walk with you and enjoy the evening?"

"Suit yourself."

She is captivating, De Armon thought, *a combination of sensual woman and endearing child*. And married besides . . . the perfect situation for a single evening's entertainment.

"Your accent sounds French," she said.

"It is. I am from Paris."

"Oh? Are you in the United States on business?"

"Both business and pleasure."

She didn't object when his arm slid around her waist.

Neither did she object when, fifteen minutes later, after idle small talk, he turned her into his arms and kissed her.

"How did you know?" she asked breathlessly in her best little-girl voice when his lips lifted from hers.

"I am French," he replied, brushing his lips across her forehead and drawing her body to his. "I have a bottle of Cointreau in my room. If I cannot buy you a drink in the lounge . . ."

"No . . . I, don't know . . ."

He kissed her again with Gallic expertise. The molding of her body to his was slow but eventually complete.

"What is your room number?" He told her. "You go ahead. I'll meet you in ten minutes."

"You're sure?"

"Of course. Why?"

His full lips pursed. "Because there were other single women in the dining room. If I wait too long for you and you don't join me, they might all be gone."

She turned to face him, the moon forming a halo around the crown of her blond hair, leaving her face in total shadow.

It was a good thing he could not see her face, because his words had turned her smile into a grimace of distaste.

"I'll be there . . . ten minutes."

The Cointreau was never poured. The door was barely closed and locked behind her when she was in his arms, sensually moving her body against his.

"Hurry, we haven't much time . . . my husband . . ."

De Armon didn't reply. As far as he was concerned, the quicker the better.

First came the dress, unzipped down the side. She slipped it off her shoulders and let it roll down over her breasts. Then she allowed the cloth to fall about her hips, then lower, until she deftly stepped out of it. Her body was blushingly pink in the room's dim light, nearly the same color as the filmy bra and the mere suggestion of panties she wore.

"You're very beautiful."

"Hurry."

"Yes." He was surprised to find his fingers shaking as he removed his own clothing.

Slowly she unhooked the bra with a practiced hand, bringing the ends of the bit of lace and nylon around in front of her, then flinging it to the floor. The panties quickly followed, and she glided to the bed.

"Are you coming?"

"Yes," he replied, moving toward her, the beacon of her naked body mesmerizing him. So enraptured was he that he gave no thought to the oddity of the fact that she carried her purse with her to the bed. His eyes were too clouded with lust to see her unsnap the bag before placing it on the bedside table.

He took her roughly, without preamble, and she responded in kind. The room was quickly filled with the sounds of their passion.

"Tell me," she moaned, "tell me when."

"I will."

She broke the ampule between her thumb and forefinger, and moved the needle between his legs.

"Tell me," she moaned, "tell me when."

"I will," he rasped, and then cried out, "Now . . . Oh, my God, now!"

At his peak, she jammed the tiny needle into his flesh. He cried out his release and slumped over her, spent.

"I'm sorry, I got carried away," she gasped, still moving beneath him. "Did I hurt you with my nails?"

"Yes, but it doesn't matter," he panted. "Pain adds spice to the pleasure."

"Doesn't it though," she replied, hiding her smile in his neck.

Over his shoulder, she checked the face of the jeweled watch on her wrist. The first stage would take about five minutes, the second and last, anywhere from five to ten minutes more.

"Is something wrong?"

"No . . . yes, I just feel a little weak."

He wouldn't admit it to her, but he felt very weak and clammy. He shouldn't have had that second brandy after dinner.

"Excuse me," he said.

He went into the bathroom, where he ran cold water into the sink. He grabbed a washcloth from the rack in the shower, made a compress, and held it to his head.

Somehow, as he staggered back into the room, he knew it wasn't the alcohol that was making him ill.

She was standing by the bed, fully dressed.

"You're leaving?" His voice sounded far away, as if it were coming from the far end of the universe.

"Soon," she replied, pulling on a pair of white surgical gloves.

"What are you doing?"

"Being sanitary," she said with a laugh. "You look better. Do you feel better?"

"I'm fine."

Suddenly a wracking pain shot through the center of his chest. He clutched himself, spun, and fell on the bed.

Marga watched the color in his face turn to a bluish hue.

She checked her watch. Only a few more minutes.

The more he gasped for breath, the less color he retained. When his face was chalky white, Marga knew he was immobile.

She started by searching the luggage and then the room. She found the four film cans within minutes but continued to make a thorough search just in case he had been more clever than she supposed.

At the end of an hour, Romar de Armon was quite dead of a heart attack, and Marga was slipping from the room.

She moved through the shadows of the trees to the bay, then retraced her steps in the full light from the bungalows back to the lobby.

"Would you like your car now, ma'am?"

"Yes, please." When the Jaguar arrived, she placed a bill in his hand and smiled. "You were quite right. It's a lovely evening."

She roared out of the drive, turning back toward Baltimore and Washington.

Dawn seeped over Chesapeake Bay in the distance. They lay, huddled on a chaise on the terrace outside their room, naked beneath blankets against the morning chill. The heated water of the pool gave off a swirling mist that eddied to nothingness by the time it reached the top floor of the hotel and the level of Carter's eyes.

"You awake?" she mumbled into the warmth of his neck.

"Umm-hmm."

"So am I . . . and sore."

"I take that as a compliment." He extinguished his cigarette and returned his hand beneath the blanket to cover her breast.

"Ummmm." She breathed, swelling the globe to fill his hand, and turned her lips up to plant a light kiss on his jaw. "You need a shave."

"We've been at it all night." He grinned. "Don't you know sex makes the beard grow?"

"I thought that was a myth. Want to go for a swim?"

"No."

"It would be the only place we missed," she said, chuckling and making the breast in his hand quiver. There were several moments' silence before she spoke again. "Want to go to bed . . . to sleep?"

"Can't. Have to meet my two associates at eight o'clock in the coffee shop."

"I'm hurt."

"How so?"

"I thought we came down here for the sole purpose of seduction. Now it turns out it's really business."

Carter smiled. "No big business. Just a little meeting I have to arrange tonight. I'll rejoin you by ten o'clock."

He moved slightly so he could look down at her. The night had removed most of her makeup and left her hair a tangled mane. He somehow liked her better *au naturel*, with the wrinkles around her eyes and her red hair unkempt and wild.

"Beautiful, aren't I?"

"Very."

Another long silence.

"Nick . . ."

"Yeah?"

"What do you do?"

A quivering ripple went through Carter's whole body. "I'm a reporter for Amalgamated Press and Wire Services."

"I don't think so."

"Oh? Why?"

"Reporters don't get so scarred up."

"Depends on what they're reporting," he replied with a laugh, and shifted the conversation to her. "What do you do over at the Securities and Exchange Commission?"

"I'm an investigator. I dig into corporations' files with my little computer and expose their shenanigans to the world."

Carter whistled. "You don't look the type to be a financial sleuth."

"I just look like a dumb redhead. Actually, I'm very smart . . . M.B.A. Harvard."

"If I ever get rich, I'll have you handle my money. Let's go to bed."

"To sleep?"

"Of course not."

But they did sleep until the telephone brought him instantly awake.

"Carter?"

"Yeah."

"Irv Pauling, CIA disbursements."

"Oh, Jesus," Carter moaned, checking his watch. It was eight-thirty. "Sorry I'm late."

"Don't worry about it. We're over at the Yankee Clipper Hotel. It had the only rooms we could get last night."

"I'll be over there in a half hour."

"Better make it quicker than that. One of the maids over here discovered a heart attack victim in his room about twenty minutes ago."

Carter's mouth went dry. Pauling wouldn't be calling to tell him about just any heart attack victim.

"Our pigeon?"

"You got it. Romar de Armon."

THREE

The gloom was oppressive in the Dupont Circle office of David Hawk, head of AXE. Adding to the depression was a gray cloud of smoke that curled ceilingward, nonstop from the man's cigar.

Besides Carter and Hawk, Bob Sievers was present, as well as the agency's West Africa expert, Phillipe Nolo.

Nolo held the floor beside a screen with a remote control slide changer in one hand and a pointer in the other. The curve of Africa's west coast, from Congo to Senegal, was on the screen, and Nolo's pointer was on tiny Togo.

"Togo, once Togoland, is bounded on the north by Burkina Faso, on the east by Benin, on the south by the Bight of Benin and the Atlantic Ocean, and on the west by Ghana. The capital is Lomé, here on the ocean."

Nolo stopped, sipped from a glass of water, and smiled. "I trust you all are still awake?"

"Barely," Hawk growled. "Get on with it."

"Certainly. As you can see, Togo is a thin strip of land three hundred forty miles long, extending inland from the ocean, and seventy miles wide. Relative to its neighbors, it has little landmass, and even less strategic importance or financial value.''

Again Hawk's voice boomed through the room. ''Then why the hell would Moscow fool with it?''

''From our reports,'' Sievers interjected, ''they got involved because the offer was made. Simple as that.''

''And every time they move, we have to countermove,'' Hawk nodded. ''Go ahead, Nolo.''

''The principal language is French. There are approximately twenty-one ethnic groups, but the country is controlled by only two: the Ewe in the south, and the Kabye in the north.''

''Enough of that, Nolo. What about politics?''

''When the current president, Jacques Goulanda, took power, political parties were banned and all constitutional processes were suspended. Even though the country has drifted toward socialism, until now there have been no hints of any catering to or from Moscow. Here is a list of other potential strong men in the Goulanda government.''

Nolo passed papers among the other three men, killed the projector, and sat down. Hawk turned the lights up from a console on his desk.

''All right,'' the head of AXE rasped, ''what have we got?''

Sievers started. ''Autopsy on De Armon indicates a heart attack. His past medical records show no history of a heart condition. Quite the opposite—the man was in fine physical shape. Heart attacks can happen, of course, and suddenly. But we must remember the Bulgarian umbrella murders in London. Tenin leaves no trace after it paralyzes the heart muscle.''

''Okay, let's assume that De Armon was terminated and that he did have the agreement he claimed. That someone picked up on him and that the agreement was for real. Could President Goulanda be playing games with Moscow?''

''Highly unlikely,'' Sievers replied. ''He might be something of a dictator, but he has no love for the Russians. If something is going on, it's probably with someone on this list.''

Hawk turned to Carter. ''N3?''

''State, of course, claimed the body. Only identifying marks were nail scratches on the buttocks. They were recent, before his death.''

''A woman?'' Hawk ventured.

Carter shrugged. ''From what we can learn of De Armon's past, he certainly wasn't in bed with another man. Chances are, if there was an agreement, he had it on film. There was a very expensive Tripon miniature camera in his briefcase. Also a receipt in his wallet for four rolls of special high-speed film purchased in Paris.''

''But no film,'' Sievers added.

Hawk fell silent, cigar smoke wreathing his head for several moments before he spoke again.

''It could be crap, but then again it could be a coup. If they want to overthrow each other, that's their problem. If Moscow is in on it, we need to know, no matter how small the damned country is. Carter . . .''

''Yes, sir?''

''I think you should go in . . . nose around, see what you can come up with. Stay in close touch. Nolo?''

''Sir?''

''What have we got down there?''

''It is, needless to say, a very small station. We have only two people, a husband and wife team, Jules and Georgette Albinzar. She is a photographer, and he works in the Hôtel de la Paix Cordiale casino. They were alerted when de Armon first approached us, and have been on it ever since.''

''Good. Do what you can, N3, but keep it dry. If Moscow is in, we just want to know.''

Without a reply, Carter stood and walked into the outer office.

The glossy dark head of Hawk's right hand, Ginger Bateman, was bent over her desk, her hands sorting documents. At the sound of the door closing, she looked up with a smile.

"I see thunder in your terrible eyes."

"Africa is not my beat. The man has decided I'm Togo bound. I'll need—"

"Tickets on the shuttle to Kennedy," she interrupted, lifting the documents one by one from her side of the desk to his. "At Kennedy, you connect with Air Afrique Flight Fifty. It flies to Abidjan in the Ivory Coast, with one stop in Dakar, Senegal. You have a one-hour layover in Abidjan before you take Air Afrique Four-forty-three on into Lomé. You have reservations for an unlimited stay at the Hôtel de la Paix Cordiale. It looks like a pretty hotel. I think you'll like it."

"Thanks a lot," Carter groaned. "Any cover?"

"You're traveling under your own name and passport, but here are credentials as a phosphates buyer for Titanlium Ltd. of London."

"Anything else?"

"Yes. How are your yellow fever and cholera inoculations?"

"Oh, God."

Her smile grew wider. "Check with the infirmary. Have a nice trip."

General Izak Tebessa paced the villa's great room like a lumbering black bear, now and then pausing to gaze down at the courtyard or out to the sea beyond.

He was a massive man, with broad shoulders made even wider by the rank boards on his uniform tunic. The tunic was opened to reveal a barrel chest under a crisply starched brown shirt, a flat stomach, and narrow hips.

Tebessa was a scholar, a soldier, and an athlete. He kept his mind and his body in trim shape for what he considered the march toward his destiny: the ruling of his country.

The long, angular black face pinched in a scowl and the

even blacker eyes flashed as an aide entered the room. "He's here?"

"*Oui, mon général*. At the gate."

"Alone?"

"*Oui, mon général*."

"Make one more sweep of the house before you let him in, to make sure all the servants are gone. And, Avilar . . ."

"*Oui?*"

"Search the bastard. This could all be part of an assassination attempt."

"*Oui, mon général*."

The aide left, and Tebessa moved to the bar. His hands were steady as he poured the brandy. As he raised the snifter to his nose, he loosened the clip on the belt holster at his side. As he drank, he checked with his eyes to make sure a second pistol was in its usual place beneath the bar.

He heard movement in the hall below, and remembered the phone call earlier that morning . . .

"General Tebessa, my name is Sir Howard Doyle. I represent Cyclops International of London."

"Monsieur, this is the Office of National Defense. I think you want Finance or Foreign Affairs."

"Quite the contrary, General. I want you. I have information that has a direct effect on Togo's national security . . . highly important, classified information."

"Very well. I can see you at . . . uh, three this afternoon."

"No, General."

"See here, Sir Whoever-you-are, let me remind you—"

"Let *me* remind *you*, General, the information I have comes directly from the safe of your ambassador to France, Jorge Bondawa. I think it would be better if we met very privately . . . perhaps this evening, in your villa outside the city?"

Tebessa had hung up the phone, cold sweat staining his uniform shirt. He looked down and noticed that his fresh shirt, one that he had donned only a half hour before, was darkening with perspiration.

"General Tebessa?"

He looked up to see a tall, distinguished-looking man in a conservative suit. His face bore the lines of about sixty years, and his black hair was streaked at the sides with gray. He had penetrating blue eyes that looked neither friendly nor unfriendly.

"I am General Izak Tebessa."

"How do you do, General? Sir Howard Doyle at your service."

"I doubt that," the general replied. "What do you want?"

"Business, General. My firm, Cyclops International, very much wants to do business with you."

"Go to hell."

"Cyclops is very powerful."

Tebessa pulled the French model F1 from its holster and jacked a 9mm shell into the firing chamber. He clicked off the safety and leaned forward to grind the barrel against the other man's forehead.

"There is no power greater than the ability to send someone to hell."

"Quite true," Doyle replied, blinking only once before smiling the suave, unruffled smile of the undaunted Englishman. "But before you kill me, I would very much like you to read something. May I open my briefcase?"

"Slowly, very slowly."

Doyle unlatched the briefcase and drew out a manila folder. "Here you are."

"Step back."

"Of course. Could I trouble you for a drink?"

"No. Sit down."

Tebessa opened the folder and began to read.

Of course it wasn't possible for a black man's face to turn white, but Doyle noticed that by the time the general finished the last page he was a few shades lighter and his shirt was soaked with sweat.

"Where did you get this?"

"From the safe of Jorge Bondawa in Clichy, outside Paris."

"It is a fake! I have enemies who—"

"I'm afraid not, General," Doyle replied, leaning back and lighting a cigarette. "Both your and Bondawa's signature, as well as those of the two gentlemen from Moscow, have been carefully authenticated."

"It is a trick, a deception!" Tebessa blustered. "I will have Bondawa arrested!"

"I think you would do better having him killed to keep his mouth shut. But even that would do you little good. We have people ready at this minute, standing by with copies to be delivered to President Goulanda, your ambassadors to the United States and the U.N., and your chief rival in the army, General Yaddo Omegla. May I have that drink now?"

The starch went out of the big body. He waved an arm toward the bar, crossed from behind it, and slouched into a sofa.

Doyle chose a good scotch and poured.

"We don't have all the details down to the minute, of course, but from the intelligence our people have gathered, I think we have pretty well pieced together the coup you and your two brothers have planned."

Doyle let the liquid roll around on his tongue before continuing.

"This is Wednesday. Friday morning, President Goulanda and several members of his cabinet will fly to Khartoum for a meeting of the OAU. At this moment, two Russian freighters are steaming toward Lomé with advance missiles and other new arms. They will land those arms at noon Friday, just as the coup starts here in the capital. With any luck the country should be yours by five o'clock, whereupon you will announce to the world that you are the new president for life. You will also announce a treaty with the Russians. Isn't that true?''

Tebessa's breath was coming in heavy gasps now. His eyes, as he rolled them up to face Doyle, were dull.

''Yes, it is true.''

''What are you giving the Russians?''

''Training bases for guerrillas, to spread revolution along the coast and up into Volta and Nigeria.''

''Stupid.''

''What?'' A flash of anger, but weak.

''You are stupid, General. In two years the Russians will depose you with another coup and put someone in they can bully. My company wouldn't do that.''

''Your company? . . . This Cyclops?''

''Yes. You see, General, we want you to go right ahead with your coup. Only instead of the Russians, we will finance you. And I am sure that you'll find we drive a much easier bargain.''

''You're mad! Do you think you can buck the Russian bear?''

Doyle laughed. ''We won't have to, but believe me, General, we could. Is your Moscow liaison still here in the city?''

''Yes.''

''Have him arrested and brought here. Then have him stop the freighters, and contact Moscow telling them that the deal is off.''

''What do you want, Sir Howard Doyle?''

''Just a few . . . minor things, such as control of your banks.''

''But why?''

''Let us say, General, that Cyclops International is having a few public relations problems. It behooves us at this time to find a new home with less business restrictions. And what better business climate than a country where we make the laws? A bargain, General?''

"Do I have a choice?"

"Of course." Calmly, Doyle picked up the second pistol from beneath the bar and crossed to Tebessa. "You can use this."

FOUR

Get acquainted with vibrant Togo as you visit the Grand Market, Arts Street, old Be Square, Independence Place, and the National Museum housing native musical instruments!

Carter sighed as he slipped the travel folder back into the seat pocket.

Seeing old three-string git-fiddles and ancient tribal drums would probably be all he would see.

It was a screwy mission, hanging on the word of one man, now dead, who had probably never told the truth once while he was alive.

"You didn't like your breakfast, monsieur?"

"What? . . . Oh, yes, it was fine. I always lose my appetite at dawn. I would like some more coffee though."

"Certainly. We'll be landing at Lomé in about twenty minutes."

The stewardess bustled away and Carter lit a cigarette.

What was the agreement between some powerful figure in Togo and the Russians? And who was the figure?

Carter had memorized the list of potential strong men in Goulanda's government from the list Nolo had provided. He had also gone over in minute detail the thumbnail sketch on each man.

Any one of them had potential.

The coffee came. He sipped it, smoked, and kept his mind working.

Where had de Armon photographed the agreement? Probably Paris.

There was only one man in France connected with the Togo government: the ambassador, Jorge Bondawa. He was being watched at that very moment. Carter figured that if he struck out in Togo, he could retrace de Armon's steps to Bondawa and try to get a peek himself at the original agreement.

But even if he did, would he be in time to head off what looked like a coup?

The landing was rocky, but no one seemed to mind. Besides Carter, there were only five other passengers deplaning at Lomé. He grabbed his garment bag and took the tail end of the line.

There was no concourse, just a walk over hot asphalt to a small terminal building. Baggage claim was just inside the door, with customs a few steps beyond.

As Carter waited, he scanned the larger area beyond the barricade. It wasn't teeming with people, so it was fairly easy to spot Georgette Albinzar. She was a tall, raw-boned woman with mahogany skin and stern, classical African features. She was dressed in a long native gown, and had a camera bag and two cameras looped around her neck and shoulders.

As each arriving passenger cleared customs and emerged from the narrow chute, she snapped his or her picture.

Carter heard her high sing-song voice as she handed each a chit: "Welcome to Togo! If you wish a souvenir photo of your arrival, just sign this and leave it at your hotel desk!"

Snap.

"Welcome to Togo . . ."

Her eyes met Carter's between snaps. They said, "Be cool," and she accented it with a slight shake of her head.

It didn't take long for Carter to see why. One was a flat-faced white man in a heat-rumpled suit right behind her.

His heavy jaw chewed on an already mangled cigar, and his eyes barely glanced at the paper in front of his face. They were too busy scanning the arriving passengers.

To his left, a short, dapper black man played at scanning magazines in a rack. His eyes also observed the passengers, but at the same time, they didn't miss a trick from the man behind the paper.

Carter guessed it was a case of spy versus spy. It was a pretty good chance that the two of them weren't on the same team.

"The purpose of your visit to Togo, Mr. Carter?"

"Business. I'm checking out some possible phosphate purchases."

The entry visa stamp came down with a thud and his passport was returned.

"Have a pleasant stay in Togo."

Snap.

"Welcome to Togo. If you wish a souvenir . . ."

Carter accepted the blue and white chit for his photo, and moved on without catching the rest of the spiel.

He spotted a men's room sign, and was heading in that direction when they came around the corner. There were five of them, four enlisted men with an officer in the lead.

They marched in step, they looked grim, and they were coming right at the Killmaster.

He tensed. In the lead-lined false bottom of his garment bag rested Wilhelmina and Hugo, his 9mm Luger and a deadly little stiletto.

He was just making up a story about the perils of traveling unarmed in Africa, when they moved on by him as if he weren't there.

He kept heading toward the men's room, glancing over his shoulder.

The spy behind the newspaper was hauled unceremoniously to his feet and, with hardly a pause, hustled from the terminal.

The watcher by the magazines smirked and moved away.

Carter sidled into a booth, dropped his bags, his pants, and sat.

Carefully he peeled the cardboard photo chit apart. The message was written on the inside of the top half: *All manner of things breaking, but hard to get a handle on the reasons. Call this number, 941-445, to order your photo. Most foreigners being followed. G.*

Carter caught an aging taxi for the three-mile ride into Lomé. He had already spotted the tail, two men in a green Renault.

At the hotel, one of them walked into the lobby right behind him. While Carter checked in, the man dawdled over a rack of brochures.

As Carter moved behind the bellman to the elevators, the man moved to the desk. Just before the door closed completely, Carter saw him examining a passport.

The Killmaster was pretty sure it was his.

In the room, he dialed the number direct.

"Yes?"

"Carter."

"This is Georgette Albinzar."

"You made a pretty fast trip from the airport."

"I am still at the airport. This is a call box. What room are you in?"

"Six-twelve."

"Eleven o'clock. Don't leave your room in the meantime."

The line went dead.

He didn't know how well trained an agent Georgette Albinzar was, but he didn't like the nervous quiver he heard in her voice.

Working with nervous backups was a good way to die.

Colonel Ivan Selevanov stood, his suddenly florid face gleaming with perspiration. He was flanked by two uniformed officers, their hands hovering over their pistols.

General Izak Tebessa sat before him, behind his desk reading from a prepared memo. Selevanov could not believe his ears.

". . . Therefore, in light of this betrayal, all foregoing agreements both oral and written between myself and the government of the USSR are null and void."

"General, this is preposterous!" Selevanov wheezed. "I swear to you there has been no leak on our part!"

"Then what do you call this?" Tebessa shouted, throwing a copy of the agreement in the KGB man's face. "I have it on good authority that the copy you have in your hands came directly from the Russian embassy in Paris."

"Impossible!"

"I am afraid not. I have already sent word to your ship to turn back. Quarters have been readied for you and your four men . . ."

"Quarters?"

"Detention quarters," Tebessa replied, "for your safety until after the revolution has taken place. Take him away."

"You will regret this, General! My government—"

"Selevanov, I have had all the threats I need for one day. Get him out of here."

The KGB colonel was half dragged, half carried from the room. The door had just closed behind him when Sir Howard Doyle appeared from behind a screen.

"Excellent, General, excellent." Doyle checked his watch. "Our trucks should be at the Ghana frontier at this very moment. By nightfall your people will be completely armed."

Tebessa sat back and lit a cigar. For the first time in hours he felt at ease. The deal he had worked out with this man and his company was indeed far superior to the one he had previously accepted from the Russians.

Also, Sir Howard Doyle had proved to him how much greater his cut of the profits would be under Cyclops than with Moscow.

"There is the remainder of our agreement, Sir Howard

. . . the Bondawa situation?''

"Of course. This phone is safe, I assume?"

"Very."

Doyle's finger quickly dialed. It was answered at once.

"Good morning, sir. Doyle here."

"Good morning, Sir Howard. Are we on our way?"

"Well on our way. In fact, only the final stroke is needed. There is that one request from the general I mentioned earlier."

"Of course. Bowldor is standing by on site. The device has already been planted. It needs only activating."

"Activate," Doyle said.

"Consider it done. Good day, Sir Howard."

"Good day to you, sir."

Doyle replaced the phone and nodded at the general with a beaming smile.

Tebessa sighed with relief and returned the smile. Jorge Bondawa was the only man in the world who was an eyewitness to his signature on the document. With him out of the way, the Russians could leak their copy all they wanted. It would be his word against theirs, and who in the world believed the Russians?

General Tebessa was beginning to like this Doyle chap.

Any man who could order another man's death with such a charming smile on his face was General Tebessa's kind of man.

The knock was three quick taps, quickly followed by her voice. "I have your photos, sir."

Carter cracked the door and she slipped inside.

"You were followed from the airport?"

"Yes."

She nodded. "I spotted him downstairs. He is a member of General Tebessa's nonexistent secret police."

"Do you suppose Tebessa is our man?" Carter said, guiding her to a chair and pouring coffee.

"He has to be. Jules is able to hear a lot over the casino tables in the evenings. In the last month, the rift in the younger officers corps has widened considerably between Tebessa and General Yaddo Omegla."

"How does Omegla fit in?"

"He is very loyal to President Goulanda. That alone would remove him from suspicion. But one other thing points to Tebessa—the Russians. At least, up until now."

"Explain."

"Tebessa is head of state security. His people check and record every person who comes into the country. Five Russians have entered Togo in the last two weeks. We have a girl in the records office. The Russians have no entries."

"Only Tebessa would have the clout to do that."

"Exactly. But as of this morning, there are different kinds of ripples. You saw that arrest at the airport?"

"I did. I thought for a moment they were coming for me."

She dropped a picture on the table between them. "He is one of the Russians."

"And he was arrested by Tebessa's men?"

"It would seem so. Four of the five were arrested this morning. The fifth was taken from his hotel by uniformed officers minutes ago. Jules is following them now."

"I didn't recognize the one at the airport. Do you have photos of the other four?"

Georgette quickly spread out four other photos. Carter latched onto one of them immediately.

"You know him?" she asked.

"Yes. His name is Ivan Selevanov. He's a KGB colonel but not a very highly esteemed one. Most of his assignments have been in North Africa as a liaison man. He twiddled his thumbs a lot with the Cubans in Angola. We suspect he was one of the reasons the Angolan operation got so screwed up."

"He's the one Jules is following now. I gave him your room number. He'll call us here."

"What else have you got?"

"About Tebessa. Jules plays a little game with the general's personal pilot. They have become drinking buddies. When the pilot plays at Jules's table, he wins. They use the proceeds for nights on the town."

"And . . . ?"

"And a week ago today, Tebessa flew secretly to Paris."

"That's it!" Carter rasped. "He flew to Paris to sign the agreement with the Russians!"

"Then why arrest the Russians in Togo?"

"That's the sixty-four-dollar question. Do you have pictures of all the other arrivals for the last month?"

Georgette nodded and dived back into her bulky bag. "We've identified most but not all of them."

"Run 'em by me."

One by one she passed the photos across the table, commenting on each.

"Schoolteacher from Chicago . . . Citroën representative, Paris . . . don't know . . . don't know . . . Moroccan diplomat . . . executive, Cyclops International . . . don't know . . ."

Carter divided the photos into two piles: study, and check later.

But his eyes kept darting to the telephone, wishing Jules Albinzar would call. Once he did, perhaps Carter would know if the Russians were in or out.

Jorge Bondawa blanked out the sounds of his wife's drunken snoring from the bedroom and concentrated on his aide's voice on the phone.

"I have the telex decoded, sir. It's marked Urgent."

"Read it," Bondawa said, buttoning his shirt with the phone cradled to his neck.

"'Urgent you destroy all papers, notes Paris meeting. Repeat urgent. New preparations being made Pres. Goulanda trip. Instruct you return Togo at once for briefing. Tebessa.'"

"Is that all?"

"Yes, sir. Is there a reply?"

"No, I'll be in the office in an hour."

"Yes, sir."

Bondawa replaced the phone and went into the study. He took not only the original of the agreement, but all the papers from the safe and returned to the living room. When they were piled neatly in the fireplace, he lit the whole and watched it burn.

When only smoldering ash remained, he returned to the bedroom. Quickly he packed a bag and slipped into his coat.

Pausing at the door, he looked back at the figure of his slack-jawed wife sprawled across the bed. He thought of writing her a note but dismissed it.

She probably wouldn't miss him anyway.

Outside, he threw his bag in the back seat of the Mercedes. In the driver's seat, he lovingly ran his hand over the expensive leather.

His and Mulata's little extravagances had very nearly cost him his career. It was a lucky thing Tebessa had come along with his plan for a coup when he did.

It was only a matter of a few more weeks before General Omegla would dig deep enough and find out just how much money had been siphoned away from Togo's foreign investments.

Bondawa turned the ignition key and felt a tremendous burst of heat beneath him just before the parts of his body separated from each other.

FIVE

He tried but found it impossible to avoid all the potholes in the narrow dirt road. There were too many, and each time the wheels of the motor scooter dropped into one, the bones in Jules Albinzar's thin, wiry body seemed to rub against each other.

Once he had gotten the direction the big sedan was taking, Albinzar had dropped back. He was able to follow the car now by its dust trail.

Two more turns and he was able to drop back even farther.

This was a secluded area of Togo's marshy southern coast. There were several villas, most of them belonging to the few wealthy citizens of the country, or high-ranking government officials.

Albinzar knew each villa and its owner. When he was sure the sedan's destination was the villa of General Tebessa, he pulled off the road and started across raw land parallel to the beach.

Five minutes later he hid the scooter in dense, marshy shrub and struck off toward the villa on foot. It was slow going to avoid being seen from the road on his left or the private lane that led to the general's residence.

At last he found the spot he needed. It was in a small grove of fat date palms and jacaranda trees on a slight elevation about three hundred yards inland from the villa.

47

Albinzar settled in and adjusted the binoculars to his eyes.

The villa was a rambling two-story affair with a large courtyard on the side facing Albinzar. Several uniformed soldiers lounged near two black Citroën sedans. Off to the side, a sandy-haired white man in a lightweight, well-tailored suit sat behind the wheel of a small Renault.

From the license plate, Albinzar knew the Renault was a rental.

Each of the soldiers at one time or another shot glances at the civilian, but there was no attempt at conversation.

Sweat ringed Albinzar's collar and dripped off his face. Lowering the glasses, he mopped his forehead, cheeks, and chin, and then cleaned the lenses. He would have loved a cigarette, but in the still, clean air the smoke would have been a beacon.

Movement at the villa's entrance brought the binoculars back to his eyes.

It was the Russian, flanked by two big uniformed officers. They manhandled him into the back of one of the sedans. Two of the soldiers jumped into the front, and the car backed around.

Albinzar followed its dust cloud. He was only mildly surprised when the car turned right on the main road toward the Benin frontier instead of left toward Lomé.

From the soldiers' treatment of the Russian, it was obvious to Albinzar that his meeting with General Tebessa had not ended on a friendly note. That would further foul up their intelligence. He and Georgette had pretty much come to the conclusion within the last few days that there was definitely something going on between Moscow and Tebessa.

Now Jules Albinzar wasn't so sure.

The little man was about to backtrack toward his scooter, when two more figures emerged from the door.

Albinzar squinted into his binoculars and frowned as the two men walked toward the rented Renault.

The tall figure of Tebessa was unmistakable. Albinzar

studied the European at Tebessa's side. He had seen that face before. But where?

And then he remembered.

The two men were all smiles, chatting and nodding to each other. At the Renault they shook hands and all but embraced.

Odd, Albinzar thought, this was what he had expected from Tebessa and the Russian. Why was Tebessa suddenly so friendly with this man?

The general was effusive toward no one who couldn't further his own ends.

Obviously the Russian was out and this man was in.

And then, in Albinzar's analytical mind, it started to make sense.

"Well, I'll be damned," he whispered, and struck off down the path.

So intent was Albinzar on piecing together what he had seen, that he went charging off the lane into the shrubbery without taking his usual precautions.

There were three of them, two soldiers and an officer. They were examining his motor scooter and jabbering among themselves.

Albinzar was nearly upon them before he skidded to a halt.

"You there! Is this your scooter?"

"Uh . . . no, I was hitching up on the road and I had to relieve myself."

The officer's eyes fell on the binoculars dangling around Albinzar's neck. His hand was halfway to the pistol at his belt when Albinzar turned and ran.

The shots came fast, three of them. Albinzar felt a tug at his left arm and the burning pain, but he kept running. He headed straight for the road until he hit the high marsh grass, then doubled back toward the beach.

Behind him he could hear their heavy boots in pursuit. There were more shots, but they were wild. Albinzar guessed they were firing to warn their comrades at the villa.

He was right. When he emerged from the tall grass and

topped the natural sand ridge to the sea, he spotted a soldier running toward him from the villa.

"Halt! Stop where you are and raise your hands!"

Albinzar stopped, raised his hands, and then bolted to his right. The beach was dotted with coves and caves all along the coast clear to Lomé. If he could get near the water and put some distance between himself and the soldiers, they would never find him.

The soldier fired.

Albinzar felt something akin to a sledgehammer slam into his back. His body was lifted. He floated gracefully through the air, then hit the sand on his side and rolled to his belly.

For a brief second he blacked out. When his eyes opened again, there was a red film over them. His left arm burned and his back ached as if a steel spike had been jammed into his spine.

By instinct his right hand crept beneath his body, then under his jacket to the Beretta in his belt. He heard the soldier's boots crunching in the sand by his feet, then felt the man's hands on his shoulders rolling him over.

Albinzar shot him twice in the face and rolled aside to avoid the falling body. Painfully he gained his feet and listened.

The others were still there, crashing through the grass trying to roust him. He got his bearings. He was about four miles from Obajuu Bay. Then another half mile up the river inland to the stilt bungalow.

His body burned like fire, but if he could steal a bicycle from one of the villages along the way, he might make it.

Slowly he moved to the rocks beyond the sand so there would be no footprints and set off, one foot in front of the other.

It was dusk, and the ocean breeze coming through the hotel room's open window was cooling quickly.

Carter sat at the bar still studying the pictures, now and then glancing up at Georgette's pacing figure.

"Something's wrong."

"Maybe they took the Russian a long way . . . inland," Carter replied.

"No. Jules would have called. He knows we are waiting."

"What do you suggest?"

"If something has happened, there is a place he would go. When we first set up here, we needed a place to store the radio and other equipment we might need for the mission."

"Of course," Carter said, nodding, "a safe house."

"Yes. It's upriver from a place called Obajuu Bay, about twenty minutes from here."

"Would you feel better if we checked it out?"

"Yes. I'll get my motorbike and meet you on the beach side . . . say, ten minutes."

She was out the door before Carter could agree or disagree.

He opened the false bottom of his bag and removed his tools. When Wilhelmina's shoulder rig was in place, he strapped Hugo's spring-release chamois sheath to this right forearm and shrugged into a lightweight leather jacket.

At the door, he paused. Something told him to repack Georgette's camera bag rather than leave it. He did, and slung it over his shoulder.

She was waiting on the beach, her long dress exchanged for jeans and a shirt, a helmet on her head. She heaved a second one out to him.

"There is something wrong."

"How do you know?" Carter asked, slipping the helmet over his head and settling into the seat behind her.

"I passed by the casino on the way out. The manager's office is right near the entrance. Two officers and two of Tebessa's secret police were just coming out. I overheard one of the officers say to the other, 'I told you I recognized him. I've gambled at his table many nights.' And that wasn't all."

"What else?"

"They mentioned my name."

"Did they see you?"

"No. I doubled back and went through the kitchen."

"Well, at least they don't have him, Georgette, or they wouldn't be looking for him. Let's go."

"Hang on!"

The rear wheel spun sand and Carter tightened his hold around her waist to keep his seat.

"Who is he and what was he doing with binoculars so near the villa?" Tebessa demanded.

"His name is Jules Albinzar, *mon général*. He and his wife Georgette emigrated from Liberia about a year ago."

"Half the damned spies in Africa carry Liberian passports!" Tebessa shouted in disgust.

"I know that, *mon général*. But other than the binoculars, we have no reason to think he is a spy. They rent a house in the Mukdan section. We have searched it . . . nothing."

"And you haven't located her, either?"

"*Non, mon général*. She has a small studio on the Rue Carmine. Her assistant says she hasn't been there since early this morning."

Tebessa ground his teeth over his cigar. The arms trucks were safely over the frontier. In a few hours the distribution would begin. In the morning Goulanda would fly out of the country.

Everything was set. Nothing could stop it, least of all a casino croupier and his photographer wife.

Nevertheless, Sir Howard Doyle had been very angry when Tebessa told him that there might have been a breach of security at the villa. Tebessa's ears still burned from the man's vehemence.

It is of the utmost importance at this juncture, General, that there be no connection between you, your coup, and Cyclops. If this should happen, withdrawal from other countries and relocation in Togo might be too awkward to contemplate.

The threat was implicit. Tebessa had lost the Russians. He couldn't afford to lose his new benefactors as well.

"Find them, Avilar. Find them and make them talk! They might be just curiosity seekers, but I must know for sure."

"*Oui, mon général.*"

The young officer marched from the room, and Tebessa reached for the ringing phone.

"Yes?"

"Doyle here, General. The matter in Paris has been concluded."

"Excellent. We move at noon tomorrow."

"May I be the first to offer my congratulations, Monsieur le Président."

Tebessa replaced the phone and belched.

Monsieur le Président Izak Tebessa.

It had a nice ring to it.

He glanced down at the execution orders his aides had drawn up earlier that day. There were over a hundred of them, and General Yaddo Omegla's name was the very first one.

It was his first official act as president.

Tebessa hummed his country's anthem as he began to sign the orders.

The house, jutting into the night sky on its spindly stilts, was dark. Carter had reconned a hundred yards downstream while the woman did the same upstream.

There were no signs of either Jules Albinzar or Tebessa's men.

Now they crouched, fifty yards from the river, in the pitch-black darkness of a thick grove of trees.

"If he were here, wouldn't he be showing a light?" Carter hissed.

"I would think so, since the house is safe. We leased it under another name before we even entered the country, and we have never even met the landlord. But . . ." She shrugged.

"Give me the layout."

"There are two wooden ladders—one on the river side, one on this side. There is only one door, this side, with a walkway around the entire house. There is only one large room, with an oil lamp hanging just inside the door."

"Okay, stay put. I'm going in."

Carter scooted soundlessly through the marsh grass and up the ladder. His feet, moving across the walkway, were like cats' paws. He bypassed the door and reached the window. There was no glass, only a battened canvas cover to keep out the weather.

Carefully he pulled the canvas open an inch and tossed a coin into the room.

Nothing.

The same operation on the river-side window brought the same results.

He used the key Georgette had given him and entered. Seconds later the lamp was lit and she had joined him.

"Where's your radio?"

"Under the floorboards over there."

"And your fastest contact?"

"Rabat, twenty-four hours."

"Get it operational!"

Carter handed her the oil lamp and moved back to the walkway. He went around the house, playing his penlight on the ground around the stilts.

Stuck in the mudbank leading from the river up to the stilts was a small fishing skiff with an outboard motor tilted rakishly off its stern.

"Georgette?" he whispered.

"Yes?"

"Does a boat come with the house?"

"No. Why?"

"Nothing, stay with the radio."

Carter had a sinking feeling in his stomach as he moved down the ladder. In the thin beam of the penlight he had seen two furrows in the mud moving from the skiff under the house.

One quick play of the light told most of the story. A cursory examination of the wounds told the rest of it.

The wounds had been serious, but if quickly and properly treated, they would not have been fatal.

He had bled to death.

"Poor bastard," Carter growled.

It was obvious that Jules Albinzar had come quite a distance after he had been shot. His clothes were saturated with blood, and there was a steady trail of it up the bank from the boat.

That struck Carter as odd. He hadn't even tried for the ladder. He had crawled directly up the bank.

Carter moved back to the body and again played his light around the corpse. The right arm was extended, the index finger of the right hand jammed to the last knuckle in the mud.

And then Carter saw why. Albinzar had been using his finger as a pencil, and it appeared that his last dying move was to make a period.

Carter moved the hand and arm. There was a word printed clearly in the mud.

CYCLOPS.

Telling Georgette was rough. He knew it would be. His guess was that Jules Albinzar was the driving force behind the team, and while she was more than competent, she was no dyed-in-the-wool, nerves-of-steel agent.

She took it stone-faced, her slender body shaking with dry wracking sobs.

Carter convinced her that the only sensible thing to do was to bury her husband immediately, near the riverbank. Reluctantly she agreed, and he found some tools and completed the sad task.

When he returned, she was on the bed, tucked into a fetal position, her eyes wide and staring.

"I know this is difficult for you," he said, gently stroking her shoulder, "but we've got to keep going. I need information."

She nodded. "I know."

"Did Jules know the Cyclops executive's name was Sir Howard Doyle?"

"No. I only found that out from his hotel this morning, just before I met you."

Her voice was hollow, lifeless.

Carter seated himself by the radio. Using Albinzar's one-time cipher pad, he had already encoded the message. When he had brought Rabat up, he sent it.

> TO: HAWK DC
>
> FROM: N3
>
> BELIEVE FIVE READ FIVE USSR NATIONALS INVOLVED TEBESSA TOGO STOP   BELIEVE TEBESSA OUR MAN BUT RUSSIANS INCLUDING COLONEL KGB IVAN SELEVANOV ARRESTED THIS DAY BELIEVE DETAINED STOP   DUE TO RUSSIAN ARREST BELIEVE COUP ON HOLD OR ABORTED STOP   AGENT JULES ALBINZAR DEAD STOP   AGENT CARTER AND GEORGETTE ALBINZAR UNDER POSSIBLE SURVEILLANCE STOP   PLEASE ADVISE OVER

Rabat cleared, and Carter turned to the woman. "Is there anything to drink?"

"Cabinet . . . there."

It was brandy, an uncorked bottle. Carter poured her a glass. She sat up and drank it listlessly.

"He was from Uganda, you know, but he became an American citizen. He came back with your CIA to fight Amin. It's funny . . ."

"What is?"

"He survived years of Amin, got me out of a jail in Kampala, and then dies in Togo."

Carter had no answers for her. He smoked and sipped the brandy for the next few hours, waiting for noise from the radio.

It came alive with the first rays of dawn.

> TO: N3
>
> FROM: HAWK
>
> ATLANTIC FLEET AIR SURVEILLANCE REPORTS HEAVY TROOP MASSINGS IN TOGO NEAR BENIN AND GHANA BORDERS STOP   ALSO REPORTS SIGHTINGS FOUR READ FOUR MISSILE EQUIPPED TANKS SIXTY MILES NORTH OF LOMÉ MOVING SOUTH STOP   YOUR SUPPOSITION NO COUP VIABLE BUT WOULD ADVISE YOU GET OUT OVER

Carter sent a "Wait," and went back to the cipher book. Three minutes later he was back on the key.

> TO: RABAT
>
> FROM: N3
>
> WILL DO STOP   SEND REQUEST ON DC ALL AVAILABLE INFO ON CYCLOPS INTERNATIONAL LTD ONE SIR HOWARD DOYLE IN PARTICULAR STOP   WILL PICK UP IN RABAT OVER

Carter shut the set down and stretched. The sun was streaming in now, and already the day's heat had started.

"Well?"

She was at his shoulder. Carter twisted to face her. She looked better. He decided to tell her all of it, including the supposition that the coup was maybe still on.

"They don't know anything about you," she said when he had finished. "Go ahead, you can get out much more easily than I can."

"No way, lady. Now, supposing the frontiers are closed,

what's the best way out of here?''

"The sea."

"I figured. Where's the best place to steal a boat?"

"The marina at Lomé, or from one of the private villas near the Ghana frontier."

"That sounds like a winner. We'll wait until dark. In the meantime . . . sleep."

Carter fell across the bed. He heard movement around the room as Georgette lowered the outside awnings to keep out the sun.

Then he felt the sag of the mattress as she lay beside him.

"Will you hold me?" she whispered.

"I'll hold you."

She moved into his arms. Slowly he felt the tenseness leave her body. When her breathing was even and regular, Carter let sleep claim him.

SIX

Carter dumped the last of the third can of gasoline on the veranda and slid down the ladder. Georgette waited with the motor scooter at the bottom.

"Better move away. When it goes, it will go big and fast."

She nodded, kicked the scooter to life, and rode about a hundred yards down the lane away from the river and the house.

Carter lit the gasoline-soaked broom, whirled it over his head, and sent it sailing up onto the veranda.

The result was instantaneous. The fire spread around the veranda and through the house. In seconds the whole thing was a blazing pyre.

Carter jogged to the scooter and settled onto the buddy seat behind Georgette. "Let's go!"

Five minutes later they bolted out of the foliage onto the road leading to Lomé. A mile or so farther on, Carter tapped Georgette on the shoulder.

"Pull over and cut the engine."

She did. "What . . . ?"

"Shhh!"

He heard it clearly now, the unmistakable chatter of small-arms fire. It seemed to be coming from the city.

"That's gunfire!" she exclaimed.

"You're damned right it is," Carter growled.

It was almost dusk. He strained his eyes to their right, inland. It was open, rolling country, but they had little choice.

"Can we skirt Lomé by going that way?"

"We can," she said, "but it will take a lot more time."

"Right now," Carter remarked drily, climbing back onto the scooter, "time may be the least of our worries."

Darkness was in their favor as they cut cross country. Now and then there was a dirt path and, only briefly, a paved road. Twice they stopped to listen and look toward Lomé.

Carter didn't need to see tanks or soldiers in the streets to know what was going on.

He and the woman were right in the middle of a revolution.

Near the Ghana frontier they cut south again. Several times they were forced to stop to avoid long columns of grim-faced soldiers.

"It's happening, isn't it?" Georgette asked. "The coup?"

"It sure as hell is. How far are we from Lomé?"

"About three kilometers from the outskirts."

When they came to a cluster of tin-roofed mud shacks, Carter called a halt. He pulled a large wad of bills from his pocket and thrust it into her hand.

"As a white man I'll stick out like a sore thumb in there," he said. "You go in, try to buy a couple of bicycles. We can't afford the noise of the scooter's engine from here on in."

Georgette nodded and slipped off into the darkness. Carter lit a cigarette and scanned the skyline toward Lomé. There were a few lights, but illumination was from several fires shooting skyward.

Obviously it hadn't been a bloodless coup.

When twenty minutes had elapsed he started to get edgy. He was preparing to move into the shantytown himself, when she appeared, pushing two bicycles.

"They're not the best," she panted, catching her breath, "but they are ridable."

"They'll do. Did you learn anything?"

"Yes." She nodded grimly. "Tebessa has declared himself president. According to a speech he made over the radio a few minutes ago, General Omegla and what's left of the army loyal to Goulanda are in retreat toward the Benin frontier."

Carter sighed. "I'm glad we didn't try to go that way."

It was slow going, but by midnight they had discarded the bicycles and found themselves near the road parallel to the beach. It was lined on the ocean side with luxury villas spaced about three to four hundred yards apart. One of five showed a light.

Far to their left, in central Lomé, they could still hear sporadic fighting.

"It seems peaceful here."

Carter nodded. "That means there are probably patrols around here keeping it that way. Which one do you think?"

"Impossible to tell. There are boat docks behind all of them. It's just a question as to which one still has a boat."

Carter knew what she meant. A lot of the owners of these villas had boats for only one reason: an escape to sea if the need arose.

"We'll just have to check them out from the seaward side. Let's go!"

In a running crouch, they crossed the road and crashed through marsh grass into an open area between two of the villas.

Carter called a halt at the beach. It looked dark and empty.

"Stay close to the grass—this way!"

He headed to his right. The first two villas were dark and appeared empty. So were their private docks.

The third was just the opposite. It was an imposing old mansion that had obviously been newly renovated. It nestled in a grove of stately palms, with a low patio wall around all four sides. A gate in the back wall opened onto a covered walkway down to the boathouse and pier.

Bobbing on lines at the end of the pier was a thirty-foot cruiser.

One problem. The villa was ablaze with light and rocking

with music and the sound of laughter.

Whoever owned it was probably a Tebessa supporter and was celebrating the coup before it was even fully over.

"We could risk going on down the beach, but we would have to go through all those lights to do it," Carter whispered. "We might as well take the bird in the hand."

Georgette nodded. "What do you want me to do?"

"Play bait, in case there is anybody on or around the boat. Turn around!"

She turned to face him. Carter unbuttoned her shirt and tucked the top into her bra. Then he tugged it from her jeans and tied the tails securely beneath her breasts. The jeans she wore were cut low on her hips.

"It will do," he said. "I'll boost you over the wall, there, at the corner. Go like hell to the gate, and then start down the walkway toward the pier as if you owned the place. If anyone is on the boat, you'll flush them."

He got his shoulder under her bottom and over she went. Staying low in the shadow of the wall, he ran in the sand to the walkway.

It was covered over the top and shielded on the sides by canvas. There were small portholes, head high, every few feet, but Carter didn't risk raising himself for a look-see. Instead he followed her progress on the planked walkway by sound.

Georgette was about twenty feet from the end of the pier and the boat, with Carter a few feet behind her padding softly in the sand, when the Killmaster heard heavy boots hit the planks.

"Who are you!" came a booming male voice.

"A servant, from the house," Georgette replied. "I just wanted to get some air."

"No one is allowed on the pier . . ."

"Oh, come on, don't you want some company down here? Do you have a cigarette?"

Good girl, Carter thought, slipping into the water and making his way under the pier. There was a ladder at the end.

He used it, and lifted his eyes just above the planked edge.

He was a tall man with a carbine slung over his back. At the moment, he was bent over cupping his hands to shield a match for Georgette's cigarette.

"How goes the battle?" she asked.

The soldier shrugged. "They probably know more up at the villa."

Georgette's light laugh filled the air. "You don't think they would tell a maid, do you?"

"No, of course not. I've heard the north is secured and General Omegla has escaped into Ghana. There is still fighting in Lomé, but it is only a matter of time. We were well prepared . . ."

He kept boasting, and once he started to turn just as Carter lifted himself to the pier. Georgette grabbed his arm, keeping him turned toward her.

Ten feet separated them. Carter made it in two steps. At the same time, he tensed the forearm muscle in his right arm. Hugo's hilt was warm in his palm as his left arm encircled the guard's throat.

The stiletto came up, under Carter's left arm and into the man's neck. Death was instantaneous, but before the Killmaster could withdraw the blade, Georgette was gasping a warning.

Carter whirled. A second soldier, incredibly huge, with a shaved, bullet head, powerful arms, and massive shoulders, was launching himself toward the Killmaster over the rail of the cruiser.

Carter moved his hand toward Wilhelmina's shoulder rig, and then stopped. A shot would probably bring more uniforms.

He would have to take this one as silently as possible with his bare hands. And that wouldn't be easy, even though Carter could see that the charging soldier had no weapon.

The giant black had Carter by eight inches and at least seventy pounds.

At the last second Carter realized that he wasn't the target of the big man's charge. He was going for his comrade's carbine, and he got it.

Just as he ripped the rifle from the corpse and came up with it, Carter reached above his head and grabbed the canopy's steel supports.

"You a dead white man," the giant growled.

Carter heaved and plowed one foot into the snout of the carbine. The butt went into the big black's gut and he went down.

But he was quicker than Carter expected. He regained the gun by the barrel and swung it like a club, catching the Killmaster in the back of the knees. Carter managed to kick out again on the way down and connect with the man's hand. Again the gun blew away, but before Carter could roll away he was covered by nearly three hundred pounds of clawing, slugging, biting animal fury.

Each punch from the black's hamlike fist was like a wrecking ball hitting his face and body.

Hand to hand it was a lousy match. But pain and anger do strange things to a man. Couple that with raw instinct and the experience of a hundred battles, and you have the transformation of Carter the man into Carter the animal.

He curled his fingers into a fist and got a straight shot into the other's throat. The black gagged, and another of the same made him gasp for air. It relaxed him enough to allow Carter to throw him off his chest.

He came up like a spring, growling, his eyes glazed. He made it to his knees when Carter's toe caught him square in the mouth. His head went back and his body followed.

Carter could hardly believe it. The huge man should have been out. Instead he crawled to one knee, shook his head, then looked up. The tribal scarification on his face, coupled with the bloody, now gap-toothed grin, was one of the most grotesque things the Killmaster had ever seen.

As if he were performing some ancient tribal ritual, he carefully picked the two teeth from his lower lip and ran a finger along the gap, gathering blood. Then his thick tongue licked the finger and the grin split his whole face.

Again the massive, bull-necked head shook and he came, crouched and powerful, like a locomotive. Carter tried to duck the charge, but the giant was quicker. With a groan from the agony in his groin, Carter hit the deck with the black on top of him again.

It felt like his guts had gone through his spine.

The black's hand went around Carter's neck. His lacerated lips dripped a steady stream of blood into Carter's face as the meaty fingers started to squeeze.

"I kill you now, white man. I squeeze your neck like a chicken's."

Carter reached up and hammered his fists into the bloodied face. The man only squeezed harder. He switched to the ribs, pounding, pummeling. He felt a couple of the black's ribs crack, but there was no letup on his throat.

The progression in the back of his eyes was from white, to blue, to purple, to red, to black. He was just passing red when he saw the barrel of the shotgun behind the black's head. Behind it was Georgette's stricken face.

No, no . . . the noise . . . ! his mind screamed.

The hammer came down with a dull click. White teeth bit pink lips as her mind worked through her face. She reversed the gun and brought it smashing down across the black's head.

He roared like a wounded bull but managed to keep his seat on Carter's chest and one huge hand around his throat. He brought the elbow of his free arm up into Georgette's belly.

She backpedaled four or five feet, dry heaving, and went down in a ball.

The giant went back to work on Carter's throat with both hands. He was doing everything by feel now. Both his eyes were swollen to slits and full of his own blood.

The respite given him by Georgette's attack had allowed Carter to get some strength back and some air into his starving lungs. But that ground was swiftly being lost again as the fingers closed tighter and tighter over his windpipe.

The Killmaster tried to buck him off, tried to ram his fingers in his eyes, tried to get to his crotch. He fought to keep the man's fingers from tightening beyond his endurance, but he felt his strength seeping away.

And then, through the red haze misting over his eyes, Carter saw the loops of two gold earrings in the black's left lobe.

He reached, curled two fingers in the small hoops, and yanked with all his strength.

The flesh held, and then gave, and they came away in Carter's hand, along with a good chunk of earlobe.

The effect was immediate. The black's hands went from Carter's throat to his own blood-spouting ear. The growl was bone chilling as the huge body rolled and wriggled on the pier like a wounded dog.

Carter struggled to his feet, took a few seconds to gasp some air, and then started for him.

"All right, you big son of a bitch," he hissed, breathing hard through clenched teeth, "you were going to kill me, were you?"

The black was on one knee, sightless, still bellowing in rage as one hand at a time struck out, trying to find Carter.

The Killmaster belted him square in the center of the face, adding a mashed nose to the ruined lips.

He fell.

Carter yanked him to a kneeling position and smashed him blow after blow with his right fist while holding him up with the left.

Blood went everywhere until, at last, Carter's left arm grew too tired to hold the weight any longer.

The huge man rolled over, still twitching, a low rattle coming from his throat. He got to one knee again before Carter drop-kicked him in the belly. As he went down again, another well-aimed kick caught him behind the ear.

Carter launched himself into the air and came down on the

man's head, all his weight on his heels. He was about to do it again, when Georgette's hands pulled him away.

"Nick . . . Nick, for God's sake . . ."

"Yeah . . . wha . . . ?" Carter panted.

"Nick, he's dead!"

Suddenly, reason returned. He wiped the sweat and blood from his eyes.

"Yeah," he rasped, looking down at the body. Then he turned to her. "Get on the boat!"

He quickly retrieved Hugo from the first guard's throat and followed her.

It was a French Chamron design powered by a four-hundred-horsepower Foursque marine diesel. The double ignition system threw him for a few seconds, but he finally figured how to cross-wire it.

"Cast off," he hissed, "bow first, and then push us around with that grappling pole."

Georgette scrambled forward, and after three tries she got the bow bouncing around in the light surf until it was headed straight out.

"Now the stern, and say when."

He didn't watch. He kept his still misty eyes on the controls.

"Now!"

"Wrap yourself around the stern rail, honey, and hold tight, I mean *real* tight!"

He hit the starter with the throttle on half, and the instant the powerful diesel roared to life, jammed the transmission into forward.

The bow leaped into the air and the cruiser left the end of the pier like a scorched cat. The bay was tiny, so they hit the breakwater in seconds. Carter eased the throttle to full and bore hard to starboard when he was sure he was free of the shoals.

By the time he made the turn, Georgette had joined him.

"How far to Abidjan in the Ivory Coast as the crow flies?" he called above the roar of the engine.

"If you keep this speed, I'd say about six hours."

"Good. We can get a direct flight from there to Rabat."

"And from there?"

Carter curled his arm around her. "Retirement for you on your husband's pension."

A shadow passed over her almond eyes, but only for a second. "And you?"

He shrugged, bending the wheel so the bow would head into a wave. "I never know."

"I'm glad."

"Of what?" he asked.

"To be out of it," she replied with a shiver.

"There's a hatch, there in the stern—opens with a pull ring. If there's any extra fuel aboard, it will be stored there. Check it out, would you?"

She moved away and was back in less than five minutes.

"Four sixty-gallon drums . . . all full."

Carter smiled.

Rabat, here we come!

SEVEN

The villa was 7,500 square feet of unbridled luxury. It lay at the tip of Cap Ferrat, descending in three tiers from the hillside down to a private beach.

One side commanded a magnificent view of the azure Mediterranean Sea, the other, the cliffs of the Riviera all the way to Nice.

From the top-floor suite, which had a 360-degree view of it all, Marcus Cologne stared down into the courtyard. Idly he clicked off the number of limousines parked there as he lit a common kitchen match and set the flame to his pipe.

Cologne was a short, balding figure with intense brown eyes and a high, scholarly forehead. Indeed everything about him, from his kindly face to his rather baggy trousers and rumpled cardigan sweater, seemed professorial, intellectual.

Nothing could have been further from the truth.

Marcus Cologne had been born fifty-seven years earlier in Palermo, Italy. His name then had been Marcello Callona, the son of a Mafia don and a woman who should have been a nun.

Childbirth had killed his mother, but that had proved advantageous to young Marcello. His father raised him in his own ruthless shadow and, recognizing early the youth's genius, had imbued him with worldly knowledge, greed, cunning, and a tremendous sense of survival.

Young Marcello made his first bones at the age of twelve. A young girl, three years his senior, had chosen a peasant boy instead of Marcello as the taker of her maidenhood.

Marcello was incensed. He found the boy, slit his throat, and then raped the girl.

Nothing came of it. His father paid the family off and the girl was sent to Rome.

Marcello honed his skill at killing—and in business—on the occupying Germans. By the time he was sixteen and the Allies had arrived in Sicily, he was adept at both.

Soon after the war he became a dollar millionaire. But the constant bloodshed among the Mafia families disgusted him. When his father was killed in one such dispute, Marcello fled to the mainland and then to Spain.

He began investing in legitimate businesses and using them for criminal pursuits. By the time he had shifted his base of operations from Madrid to London and eventually to Paris, he had amassed one of the largest fortunes in the world and had become a respected gentleman, Marcus Cologne.

Other people ran the business now—and did the killing—but nothing escaped his wary eye.

The last word always belonged to Marcus Cologne.

"Monsieur?"

"Yes, Serge?"

Bowldor stood in the open door making a conscious effort not to chomp on the wad of gum in his mouth. Monsieur Cologne hated to see his jaw work crudely in such a fashion.

"Sir Howard has arrived. They are all here . . . in the council room."

"I'll be down in a few moments."

"*Oui, monsieur.*"

Cologne turned back to the window. As he sipped from a glass of Perrier, he noticed two lithe young girls frolicking totally naked in the surf.

Nubile young bodies and good brandy were staples of Cologne's life. That is, until a few years before, when the stress of business had robbed him of such pleasures.

Now he was worth close to sixty billion dollars, and the strongest drink his stomach could handle was Perrier.

As for the nubile young bodies . . . Marcus Cologne had not had an erection in five years.

Because of a storm, the boat ride from Lomé to Abidjan took twelve hours instead of six. On top of that, there was another nine-hour wait for a commercial flight on to Rabat, Morocco. Carter's request for a charter was laughed at.

They found a hotel room in the interim. While Georgette shopped for fresh clothing, Carter called home.

It was about what he had expected. The coup was successful. Tebessa was in full control of the country. So far he had made no declarations, but as far as Washington knew, there was no hint of Russian involvement.

President Goulanda had returned from the OAU meeting in Khartoum to Dakar, Senegal, where he had asked for and received asylum.

There was more, much more, but Bob Sievers was preparing a brief on it and would meet Carter in Rabat.

Through Hawk, the Killmaster made arrangements for Georgette. Seven hours of much needed sleep followed, and then they had boarded an Air Afrique flight to Rabat.

Now Carter stood on the observation deck of Nouasseur Airport, outside Casablanca, and watched the Pan Am 747 ease away from the gate. On it was Georgette Albinzar heading for a new life and a desk job in AXE's Africa division.

Carter checked the time. Sievers and his entourage were due in on another Pan Am from Paris in thirty minutes.

He went below, got a sandwich, and glanced through the *International Herald-Tribune*.

A one-column, half-page story on page three reiterated the daring coup in Togo and the plight of the late president. Goulanda was already appealing to the U.N., the U.S., and his neighbors for arms and money to recapture his country. To date, nearly all of his appeals had fallen on deaf ears.

The end of the story was a shaded observation that under General Tebessa and military rule, Togo's economic success and human rights achievements of the past few years under Goulanda would quickly go down the tubes.

Through the restaurant's big glass windows, Carter saw the flight from Paris land.

Sievers was just emerging from customs when Carter hailed him.

"I would have met you in Paris," Carter said, shaking the man's hand.

"I know, but the old man thought you might be able to do some good here first. Have you got a car?"

"Yeah," Carter nodded. "I also made you a reservation at the Casablanca."

"We'll talk in the car."

Sievers set up papers from his briefcase on the seat between them and drove himself. The airport was twenty miles from Casablanca's city center. He took his time.

"From what we have been able to glean, the Russians are stewing."

"Then they did have a deal with Tebessa," Carter said.

"It would seem so, and apparently he reneged at the last minute."

"Brave man," Carter replied. "Quickie dictators usually get big bucks backing before they try to take over their country."

"It would appear that Tebessa did, with the Russians, but he got a better offer at the last minute."

"Is that supposition or fact?"

"A little of both. The day after the coup was solidified, Colonel Ivan Selevanov and his comrades were dumped over the frontier into Benin. They made it to Lagos and took a Lufthansa flight to Frankfurt. Our people lost them there. They probably disappeared into the East."

Carter chuckled. "Never to be heard from again. Selevanov has screwed up too many missions."

Sievers nodded and went on. "A report through Interpol from the Paris Sûreté seems to point to the Togo ambassador in Paris as De Armon's source for the original Russia-Tebessa agreement. His name was Jorge Bondawa, and his wife had a very wandering eye. She would have been easy pickings for a gigolo like De Armon."

"You say 'was'?"

"Jorge Bondawa is currently in pieces. Somebody put a bomb under his butt when he sat down in his brand-new Mercedes."

"The comrades?"

"Maybe . . . maybe not. It could be Tebessa's new backers. What led you to ask about Sir Howard Doyle and Cyclops International?"

Carter told him about the finger-written word in the mud, and about the picture Georgette had taken of Doyle arriving at the Lomé airport.

"When Jules Albinzar bought it, he was following Selevanov. But the last thought before he died was Cyclops. I'd guess that Jules spotted Doyle, probably with Tebessa."

"Probably a good guess," Sievers said, pulling into the vast parking lot adjacent to the Hotel Casablanca.

Sievers put his briefcase back together and the two men entered the hotel.

"Drink?"

Sievers nodded. "A quiet table."

The found one in the corner of the lounge. Carter ordered scotch while Sievers stuck to the North African drink, hot mint tea.

When they had been served, Sievers got right back to the business at hand.

"None of it makes a hell of a lot of sense. Goulanda is a socialist, but heavy on the democratic side and a staunch friend of the West. Tebessa is an unknown quantity other than the few pronouncements he's made since the establishment of his regime."

"Since declaring himself president for life and probably opening a few Swiss bank accounts," Carter countered.

"Exactly. Now, since the Russians were in and then out, it would figure that Doyle and an international conglomerate as big as Cyclops just might have a very vested interest in little Togo."

"How so?"

"We did a lot of digging through European financial circles and by way of your friend Yvonne Molina in the SEC. As it turns out, the lady is quite a financial detective. By coming up with Cyclops's North American business interests alone, she surfaced a lot of hanky-panky. After correllating it with what our people found out on this side of the pond, she was able to put together a very interesting scenario."

Sievers slid a bound folder across the table. It was at least five inches thick and had one word on the cover: CYCLOPS.

Carter sighed. "Can't you just give me a rundown?"

"I'd like to," Sievers replied, "but Hawk told me to have you read the whole thing. He and I have put our heads together on some conclusions. We want to see if yours agree."

"This will be at least two hours' study," Carter groaned.

"More like four," Sievers said and chuckled. "I'll meet you for dinner and we'll discuss it."

Carter had no choice but to agree, even though wading through four hours of financial statistics was a long way from his idea of action.

He agreed to meet with Sievers in the dining room later and took the elevator to his room. As per his request upon leaving the lounge, a bellman had already delivered a bucket of ice and a bottle of Chivas.

He put off cracking the Cyclops report until the tub was full of warm, soothing water and he already had three fingers of Chivas in his belly.

Then, submerged to his shoulders, cigarettes and scotch near at hand, he began to read.

Ten pages into the report he was moaning aloud, scotch and cigarettes forgotten.

Thirty pages into it, he knew he wouldn't put it down until he was finished.

Marcus Cologne walked into the villa's large conference room and greeted each of his directors by name and a handshake as he moved across the room to his own chair at the head of the table.

"General . . ."

"Marcus, it's been too long," replied the tall, straightspined man with a mane of iron-gray hair and a face that was every Hollywood casting director's dream of what an American hero should look like.

General David Pettit, U.S. Army Ret. Before he retired and became chairman of Cyclops North America, Pettit was head of the Pentagon's surplus arms and munitions division. In this capacity he was able, for years, to inform Cyclops of what to bid for millions of dollars' worth of surplus equipment. Cyclops rarely lost a bid and always found it easy to obtain the correct end-user certificates in order to sell to anyone they chose, friend or foe of the United States.

When a snoopy reporter had uncovered rumors of collusion, Cyclops's power had silenced them. The general resigned indignantly, and six months later went to work for Cyclops at ten times his army salary.

"Lars, I was so sorry to hear about your wife."

Lars Gustafsson's face broke into a smile. "Thank you, Marcus. Her accident was a pity. But then, those of us who live by the bottle will eventually perish by it."

Gustafsson's wife had driven off a bridge six months earlier in Stockholm. It was declared an accident. Actually it was murder, ordered by Marcus Cologne and carried out by Serge Bowldor as a favor to the head of Cyclops's vast shipping empire.

The woman's drinking had become a security risk, and

besides, Gustafsson wanted to marry his youthful mistress.

Henri Dumarne embraced Cologne and kissed him on both cheeks.

"We must get together a game, Henri, when this dreadful business is over."

"Of course, Marcus."

Dumarne, aside from being one of the finest chemists in the world, was also an avid golfer. He ran chemical plants all over the world. He was also overseer for the company's huge holdings of poppy and coca fields. An alternate chore for his chemical plants was the refining of much of the world's supply of heroin and cocaine.

Heinrich Keller snapped to attention, clicked his heels, and bowed slightly as Cologne passed.

Keller was once Kurt Heiss, an SS colonel who had become adept during the war at two things: leading assassination teams against the Allies, and smuggling huge sums of gold and antiques out of Germany at the end of the war.

Since he had become Heinrich Keller, his organizational abilities had been turned to forming an army of enforcers and spies for Marcus Cologne and Cyclops. If a government official anywhere in the world had a stain on his past, Keller knew it. If that official's signature was ever needed on a Cyclops contract, he was sure to get a visit from Herr Heinrich Keller.

"Sir Howard, my congratulations. You have done a tremendous job."

"Thank you, Marcus."

Sir Howard Doyle had shunned his family and his peerage almost from birth. He was an adventurer, a womanizer, a genius, and completely amoral. As such, he was the right hand to Marcus Cologne and the logical successor to the Cyclops throne.

Cologne reached the head of the table and sat. The others followed suit.

"Gentlemen, because of Keller's excellent intelligence apparatus and Sir Howard's daring, our major problems, I think, are solved. But first let us review the problems themselves. General, your report."

Pettit coughed, checked his notes, and began.

"There has been no change. The American Securities and Exchange Commission, in collusion with their Canadian counterpart, breathes harder down our necks every day. I think it safe to say that one day soon they will have enough material for an indictment. Needless to say, it will be years in the courts, with very little chance of success. But the indictment alone would severely hamper our doing business in the United States under the Cyclops banner."

".I am afraid my plants in France and Spain fall under the same cloud, Marcus," Henri Dumarne said.

"Lars, how about shipping?" Cologne asked, turning to the Swede.

"As difficult as it is to fathom, I am afraid there will be no Liberian licenses for our ships when the current ones expire. Being able to issue our own licenses, without United Nations interference, will solve our problems."

"I, too, am having constant difficulties," Keller interjected. "My agents are constantly being harassed by both Interpol and the police and security forces of every country they are in. Giving them diplomatic status would put us back in power."

Sir Howard Doyle stood and distributed copies of his report to each of the men. As he did, he spoke in a quiet monotone.

"As you are aware, gentlemen, Cyclops had already been literally kicked out of the U.K. It is only a matter of time before the other countries in the Commonwealth follow suit. That is why the move we are about to make is imperative."

Marcus Cologne accepted the brief but left it on the table before him, unopened. He had already read it and concurred with all of Doyle's findings. He waited to speak until the others had read through their copies.

"Are we sure of Tebessa, Sir Howard?"

"No doubt of it. I have already set up dual accounts for

him in Switzerland and the Cayman Islands. The initial deposit was one million American in each account.''

"Pennies," Cologne snorted.

"Quite," Doyle said, a smile curving his thin lips, "considering the return we will get by owning our own country."

Carter dropped the Cyclops report on the table and fell into a chair across from Sievers at the same time.

The State Department man's grin was enigmatic. "Fascinating, isn't it?"

"Yvonne did quite a job."

"She sure as hell did. What do you make of it?"

"There's only one thing to make of it. Cyclops is all-powerful, a maze of holding companies, sheltered accounts, hidden assets, disguised ownerships, and God knows what else. One hell of a nut to crack."

"Yes, but one thread runs through it all. They are getting kicked out of every country they currently have a base in to do business. What does that tell you, Nick?"

"It tells me that it would behoove Cyclops to buy their own country so they can make their own laws."

"Exactly. And that's what the boys in Analysis think they've done."

"What do we do about it?" Carter asked.

"Nothing."

"What?"

"It's been through State, Defense, all the security agencies, and even our U.N. representative. It's too hot. Overt or covert now would smack of open interference, too much so."

"What about Goulanda?"

Sievers shrugged. "He's got a good general, the basis for an army, a way to get more, and if he invaded, he could probably win with the right propaganda laying the groundwork in Togo."

"So, let's send him a few tanks and tell him to have at it!"

"No can do. Nobody wants to get involved, even the Russians. We've already sent feelers."

"You mean we do nothing?"

Sievers snapped his lighter and held the flame under Carter's cigarette. The Killmaster noticed the man's hand was shaking slightly.

"Wrong. *You* do something."

"Me?"

"That's right. Hawk says that of all the agents we have, you've got the best knowledge of the world's seedy and shady characters. We want you to find the money, buy the arms, and get them to Goulanda without anyone knowing about it."

Carter wheezed smoke through his nostrils. "Is that all?" he asked drily.

"That's it. We can help you with information and small things, but there must be no taint of U.S. or any Western involvement. I've an idea the Russians and their comrades feel the same way."

"Good God, man, you're asking the impossible!" Carter barked.

"Perhaps," Sievers said with a shrug. "But I think it's worth a try. Take a few days to let it sink in, and let us know in Washington." He opened the menu. "What's good here?"

"Crow," Carter growled, and signaled the waiter for a fresh drink.

EIGHT

Carter spent the next forty-eight hours going over and over the Cyclops report, as well as checking further details from Paris, London, and Washington. Almost hourly, another question impeded his progress and he would get on a special scrambler line to one of the three cities.

Sievers had made arrangements for a small villa to be placed at Carter's disposal. It came complete with a house-boy, Ismael, who had been cleared.

By the end of two days, the fog started to clear and the Killmaster came up with his needs and his options. He jotted them down in order on a legal pad:

> 1) CLARIFY AND SUBSTANTIATE THE CONNECTION BE-TWEEN TEBESSA AND CYCLOPS FOR FUTURE USE IN FOMENTING INTERNAL REVOLUTION PREPARATORY TO GOULANDA ATTEMPT TO RETAKE COUNTRY.
> 2) MONEY, UNTRACEABLE, FOR THE PURCHASE OF ARMS, ALSO UNTRACEABLE.
> 3) SECRET TRANSPORTATION OF ARMS TO MOROCCO.
> 4) TRANSPORTATION OF ARMS TO GOULANDA.
> 5) SET REVOLUTION IN MOTION.

At the end of forty-eight hours it was solidified enough so that Carter knew he couldn't do the job without help, a great deal of help.

He called Dupont Circle and got in touch with Ginger Bateman.

"I need things."

"That's what I'm here for."

"There's a guy who used to operate out of Algiers. Only name I have on him is Rollo. I think his real name is Rowland. He's a one-eyed bandit from the States. Used to be a bookie someplace in the South. He ran about three years ago."

"What do you want to know?"

"Everything we've got, and his current whereabouts."

"Will do. What else?"

"Yvonne Molina. She can help a lot. Get her on a short leave from SEC. Clear her and brief her. Then have her call me here."

"Is that it?"

"That's it. I'll be in touch."

Carter showered, shaved, dressed, and went out. Ismael's cooking was excellent, but tonight he had a yen for air and restaurant food.

The villa was located in the New Medina just above the Great Mosque. Carter shunned the car and walked down to the Boulevard Victor Hugo. His mind was still on the problem, so he only looked halfheartedly for a restaurant. After bypassing two that looked jammed, he chose a quiet, ill-lighted little café off the main street.

To his astonishment he devoured all four courses, and though he hardly ever indulged in desserts, he ordered a local rose-water-flavored pastry layered with syrup.

Over brandy, he noticed her. Dark, quite beautiful, probably a French mother and Arab father, or the reverse. She wore a two-piece number in figure-clinging jersey. It was a dark burgundy color that accented her dark features.

She made no bones about talking to him with her eyes.

Carter was tempted, but he knew "the problem" would impede his performance.

Reluctantly he finished his brandy, paid the check, and moved out into the night air. He didn't turn when he heard the click of heels moving up behind him.

"Is monsieur alone tonight?" She slid an arm through his right arm and squeezed his bicep with her free hand.

"Sadly, mademoiselle, yes. And I must stay that way."

"A pity," she replied. "My firm gives excellent tours of the city."

Carter chuckled. "I'll just bet. But I'm afraid . . ."

The feel was unmistakable. He didn't even have to look down.

She was good, very good. The revolver's muzzle was separating his sixth and seventh ribs. Two quick shots would raise hell with his lungs, and chances were good one of them would find his heart.

She had probably spotted at dinner that he was right-handed. That put his own weapon on his left side. Her left arm was like the tentacle of an octopus around his right, squeezing hard and steady.

"Silencer?"

"That's quite correct, Monsieur Carter. But I have no intention of killing you unless you prompt it."

"Then why the gun?"

"Because the gentleman who sent me to fetch you informs me that you often react quite violently to force."

"The gentleman is quite right. Who is he?"

"You shall see. Turn left here."

It was a small alley, and very dark. Two steps into it, she tugged him to a halt. A large black sedan slid to a stop behind Carter, completely blocking the alley mouth, and two squat, powerful men in stained ties and rumpled suits faced him.

The two men made it for him with their dated ties, curled collars, and sloppy suits. The girl was obviously Moroccan. The men were Bulgarians or Russians, and probably KGB.

"We wish no problem, just a quiet conference," said one of them in broken, thickly accented English.

Carter replied in Russian. "I'll think about it, but I'll think in much quieter terms if I've got a name."

The two men exchanged glances, then looked to the woman for confirmation. Carter saw her nod over the barrel of the Beretta held steadily in both hands.

"Major General Kolack Ivanovitch Mock."

Carter lifted his hands in the sign of the cross and smiled. "It will be like old times."

There was relief on both their faces as they patted him down and lifted Wilhelmina.

"He has a blade of some kind attached to his right forearm," the woman said.

One of the men reached for Carter's right cuff.

"Don't bother." He tensed his arm, and Hugo popped into his palm, the razor tip of the blade just touching the man's throat. Carter flipped it, hilt first, and dropped it into the man's quivering hand. "Shall we go?"

General Kolack Mock rose with an ear-to-ear smile and extended a beefy hand as Carter entered the room.

"Carter, we meet at last!"

"General."

"Of course we know each other's files and faces."

"Of course."

"Sit, sit. Vodka?"

"If you have some ice."

The Russian made a face but mixed the drinks. "Forgive me for the method of meeting, but it would be very unwise of me to be seen on the streets anywhere in Morocco. As you probably know, I was asked to leave Rabat a year ago."

Carter knew the story well. Mock had been military attaché to the Russian embassy in Rabat. His real title was First Directorate Liaison, and his job was spying. When the Moroccan intelligence service, with CIA help, had pinned him down as the source of military information being passed to Algeria and the sub-Saharan rebels, he had been booted out of the country.

"I had assumed you were back in Moscow," Carter said, accepting the glass of clear liquid.

"Alas, no. My current duty is even worse than Moscow.

Since I am the reigning expert on African affairs, I'm doomed to run my networks here from a freighter offshore. It's a terrible job. *Na zdorovia.*"

"*Na zdorovia.*" Carter downed the vodka and relaxed somewhat.

This was the first time he had met Mock face to face, but he knew the KGB. If Mock was volunteering his current status, Carter had been asked here to make some kind of a deal.

"Another?"

"Of course." Carter held up his glass and grinned. "Will this be a one-bottle or two-bottle discussion?"

The general roared, filled the glasses, and set the bottle between them. "You see, that is why you Americans are such poor diplomats, particularly in the Arab countries. You always must thrust to the heart of business instead of discussing the merits of the latest belly dancer, the achievements of the other man's first-born son, and what is new in the defeating of the cursed Zionists!"

"I happen to like Israel," Carter replied. "And I know I'm a lousy diplomat."

"True, but you are an excellent agent. Do you know how much Moscow has on your head?"

"A private car, a larger Moscow apartment, a *dacha* on the Black Sea, and a promotion . . . the last time I heard."

"True. You are lucky I already have all those things!" Mock chuckled, and then his broad face grew serious. "We have a squirrel in the Hôtel de la Paix Cordiale in Lomé."

Carter shrugged. "So you know I was in Togo."

"We also know that you barely got out. What we would like to know is what you found out before you escaped."

"You mean, who replaced you in Tebessa's affections?"

"Touché. Another drink on that. Who did? . . . Your people?"

"No way, and you know it."

"Who then?"

"What do I get for it?" Carter asked coolly.

The general pushed a folded piece of paper across the low table. Carter opened it. On it were eleven principal European and African cities, eleven code names, and eleven phone numbers.

"If you plan on doing something about Togo, I have been instructed to help you in any way I can."

Carter stared at the man, and then chuckled. "If you can't get in, you don't want anyone else in, right?"

"Exactly. Isn't that the way we both operate? Who is it?"

"Private," Carter replied. "An international conglomerate. They're in bad shape all over the world. They need a new base of operations."

Mock sighed. "We suspected as much. It's a pity. We had a great deal of time and money invested. Needless to say, Moscow wants revenge."

"Then perhaps we can make a deal."

Carefully Carter outlined the necessities. As he talked, the general made copious notes. By the time Carter finished, the Russian's face was screwed into an intense map of concentration.

"I must get approval from Moscow, of course, but I don't think that will be a problem. Is there anything I can provide for you immediately?"

"I'll need liaison here in Casablanca with the rebels to the south. If I can secure the arms, I'll ship them out of here."

"Easily done," the Russian said, nodding. "The woman who helped abduct you tonight, she is very good."

"So I noticed," Carter growled, remembering the speed of the gun in his ribs.

"Her name is Leila Asheem. She will be at your disposal."

Carter stood, this time offering his hand. "Just tell her that when the game is over, not to try to collect the reward."

Mock's face was as innocent as it could be. "You have my word on it."

They shook hands, and Carter turned. At the door he

paused. "By the way . . ."

"Yes?"

"Colonel Selevanov . . . ?"

"The esteemed colonel has been retired. I'm afraid we will see no more of him."

"I didn't think we would."

The phone was ringing when Carter let himself back into the villa.

"Yes?"

"Where the hell have you been? I've been ringing every fifteen minutes!" It was Ginger Bateman.

"I had a date with a bear. What have you got?"

"James Rowland, alias Rollo, alias Frank Rowland, James Rollmar, Jim Boy Rolliman, and about a dozen others. Want them all?"

"No need. Fill me in."

"In the vernacular, he's one bad dude. Tried to collect some gambling debts from the wrong people in the States. They paid him off with a year in the hospital. When he got out, he repaid the visit."

"How many?"

"Four very big biggies, and done in a very messy way. He took off for Spain, but the friends of the deceased declared enough was enough and let him go."

"Where in Spain?"

"Barcelona, Marbella, Malaga, you name it. But he was politely asked to leave."

"Where is he now?" Carter asked, doing his best to keep the edge out of his voice.

"He has a yacht called the *Long Shot*. It's registered out of Tunis, but it's rarely there. When he's not fleecing American bigshots in high-stakes poker around the French Riviera, he's smuggling to Africa and back. We haven't got a line on where he is right now."

"I might have a way of finding out from here," Carter

replied. "Put me on tape."

"You're on."

"To David Hawk with copy to Robert Sievers. From N3. Re: Togo . . ."

Carter talked for a half hour. He detailed his complete plan of attack, his conversation with the KGB general, and relayed the code names and numbers on the paper Mock had given him.

"Is that it?" Ginger asked.

"Yes. What about Yvonne?"

"She's briefed and cleared and in our computer center right now."

"Switch me over."

Ten seconds of buzzes and clicks, and the redhead's familiar voice came on the line.

"I knew you did something important!" she exclaimed.

"It's all in how you think something's important," Carter replied. "I need your help."

"You've got it. Only I wish I were there. Morocco sounds exciting!"

Carter squeezed his eyes and saw Yvonne Molina standing naked at the foot of his bed. He opened his eyes and the image was still there.

"Nick, are you still there? Did you hear me?"

"I heard you. I wish you were here, too, but I need you where you are. I need confirmation tying Tebessa to Cyclops . . . fund transfers, accounts, anything."

"Tricky, but I think I can do it. Anything else?"

"Yeah, somebody in the arms business who is legal but would be willing to sell if the sale could be shielded. No traceable end-user certificates, no transfer memos, no sales invoices—"

"In other words, no trail."

"You got it. All I need is a name . . . and preferably somebody far removed from Cyclops."

"That might take some time," she replied.

"That's okay, but get cracking on the Cyclops-Tebessa connection first."

"That it?"

"That's it. I'll check back sometime tomorrow."

"Okay. And, Nick . . ."

"Yeah?"

"The night at the bay was . . . well, it was . . ."

"Yeah, it sure was. *Ciao.*"

Carter cleared the connection and unfolded the slip of paper Mock had given him. He ran his fingers down to the Casablanca number and dialed. The phone was answered on the first ring by a very bored voice that quickly came to life when Carter spoke.

"Hometown, this is Drumbeat."

"One moment," came the reply in French.

It was more like five full minutes before Mock's voice came on the line.

"That was quick. Are you in trouble already, my friend, or have you found uses for our expertise?" the Russian asked.

"The latter. There's a big-time gambler and smuggler floating around on a sixty-five-footer called the *Long Shot*. He operates out of Tunis, and probably works Nice, the Greek isles, and both sides of Morocco. I need a location ID on him as soon as possible."

"Do you have a name?"

"He's got about a hundred of them, but try Rowland or Rollo."

"I know of the man," Mock said. "It shouldn't be difficult. Do you have a safe number, or should I call you there?"

"You mean you know this number?"

"Oh, yes, my friend. We know a great deal more than you think we do. Good night."

The line went dead.

Carter passed a bottle over a glass, then changed his mind

and poured the drink out. His bones said bed.

He was down to his pants and shorts when he heard the front door open and close, then the steady padding footsteps on the stairs.

They were heading directly toward his room.

It couldn't be Ismael. He'd left for the night and never came back before seven in the morning. Besides, the steps were too light.

He jacked a shell into the Luger's chamber and killed the lights.

The footsteps stopped right outside the door. Then there was a light rap, and Carter sighed. Killers don't announce themselves by knocking.

He flipped Wilhelmina's safety on and opened the door.

It was Leila Asheem, in the same figure-hugging burgundy dress.

"General Mock said I was to put myself at your disposal."

"How did you get in?"

"I have a key. We had it made yesterday from an impression we made when we searched the house."

Carter couldn't suppress a laugh. "Jesus Christ, the games we play."

"Well?" she said, her kohl-lined eyes boring into his.

"Well what?"

"Where do I sleep?"

"Guest room's down the hall, second door on the right."

"Thank you."

She moved away, doing marvelous things underneath the dress.

Carter closed the door, stripped off the rest of his clothes, and crawled into bed.

But he didn't sleep. He listened to the sounds from down the hall. When he heard the shower start, he thought of Yvonne. When he heard it go off, he thought of Leila.

He lit a cigarette, took two drags, and mashed it out. Two

minutes later he lit another, took three drags, and mashed it out.

"Shit," he said, plucking a robe from the end of the bed and moving down the hall.

The light was on and the door was wide open.

"Leila . . ."

"Yes?"

She stepped from the bathroom wrapped in a towel. Her hair was still wet from the shower and it clung tightly to her head in tiny curls.

"Since Mock put you at my disposal, I thought I'd put myself at your disposal."

Her smile was either the most erotic or most evil thing he had ever seen.

"I'm glad."

"Oh?"

"General Mock says you are a very dangerous man. Dangerous men excite me."

She shrugged the towel off and stood naked, with one hand on her hip, the other crossed to meet it. The effect was staggering. She had the body of a goddess, the skin flawless, creamy, and incredibly smooth from the high-standing breasts to the curved instep. An aura of total sexuality was etched in the curve of her hips, the pose of her head, and the thrust of her pelvis as she moved into his arms.

"Is this in the line of duty?" he murmured, feeling her body mold to his.

"No, this is strictly in the line of pleasure," she whispered, her lips moving softly across his cheeks, his neck, and then finding his mouth.

Carter lifted her by the hips, carried her, and then set her gently on the bed. Without a pause, she pulled him feverishly down beside her and forced his hands to her breasts.

Then her mouth was against his, hot and moist and hungry. Her tongue darted against his lips, his teeth, her hot breath flowing softly across his face. He held her tight, letting his hands run up and down her naked back, and then down her thighs, and back up.

"He was right," she moaned as Carter moved between her thighs.

"Who?"

"Mock. You are a dangerous man. Owww . . ."

"All right?"

"Yes, oh, yes . . . do your duty!"

"Marga?"

"Yes, Marcus."

"I'm afraid you'll have to go back down to Washington as quickly as possible."

"I can leave this morning."

"Fine. We managed to track down the number De Armon used at the airport in Paris. It's a private government agency line, one of several used by the State Department. Our man there was able to pinpoint its designated user."

"A man or a woman?" Marga Lund asked, lightly curling the hair over her right ear with her fingers.

"A man. His name is Robert Sievers. It seems that he has some type of liaison post between the State Department and various intelligence agencies. As near as we can ascertain, he is putting some sort of plan into operation that will affect our Africa project. We have followed him for the last five days. He made contact in Casablanca with a man we believe to be an agent."

"Is Sievers to be terminated?"

"I'm afraid so. We'll take care of the agent from this end. Hopefully, if we bite off the two heads of the snake, it will take a sufficient amount of time for the body to grow more. By then we will be established in Lomé."

"Do you have any characteristics?"

"The address is Forty-one-thirteen Leeds in Georgetown, and he does have a habit of stopping every morning at a small tobacco and newsstand near his flat. And Marga . . ."

"Yes, Marcus?"

"Do make it appear to be an accident."

"Don't I always, Marcus?"

"Of course you do, my dear. I'll look forward to seeing you at the villa next week. Good-bye, my dear."

"Good-bye, Marcus."

NINE

It was about a ten o'clock sun that split the bedroom drapes and slanted across their bodies. Carter popped one eye and rolled it to the side.

Leila Asheem was lying on her side, facing him, sleeping softly, her breasts cradled in her arms.

He was about to touch her, when the bedside phone rang, bringing her instantly to an upright position. Her body was tense and her right arm poised to strike as she shook the clouds of sleep from her mind.

"Easy, it's me, remember?" Carter murmured. "We're on the same side . . . for now."

She smiled and slumped back to the pillow. "I remember. Your phone is ringing."

"Yeah." He reached for the jangling instrument. "Carter here."

"Good morning." It was Mock.

"Morning, General."

"Did Leila arrive?"

Carter shot a look at the bed. The sheet had slipped to her navel. She lay on her back with one arm thrown over her eyes. Her steady breathing made her chest rise and fall in an erotic way.

"Yeah, she arrived."

"Good. My people have located your man. He anchored in the Port of Monaco two days ago. He plays golf in the afternoon and entertains on his yacht in the evenings."

"Will he stay there for a while?" Carter asked.

"It would appear so. There is a lot of Mideast and American oil money there right now. It seems to be a rather off-the-cuff convention of some kind. There is a woman, Angela Picard, who steers a lot of the fat wallets to him each evening."

"How can I find her?"

"She scouts new blood at the chemin de fer tables each night at both of the casinos."

"Many thanks, General. I'll let her find me."

"Good hunting, my friend."

Carter hung up and headed for the bathroom.

"You're not sexy in the mornings?" Leila called from the bed.

"Not after a night like last night," he said over his shoulder as he stepped into the shower.

He almost laughed out loud when he stepped out onto the terrace a half hour later. Ismael had set the breakfast table for two.

How the little man knew, Carter could only guess. The food arrived within seconds after Leila had slid into the chair opposite him.

"Will madame be staying for dinner?"

"Madame has moved in, Ismael, for the run of the operation."

"*Oui, monsieur.*"

The dark little man disappeared, and Carter flattened a map between them.

"When I get the arms we need into Casablanca, I want to take them through rebel country overland, here, through the western Sahara."

"That means contacting the Marxist rebels in the south," she commented. "You'll be going right through their territory."

"Right," he replied. "That's your job. Also, find me a quiet place on the coast to load. We'll take them by sea around the coast to a night landing somewhere in Ghana."

"You have ships?"

"I'm flying to Nice this evening to meet a man who can arrange for them."

She nodded. "I will have everything ready by the time you return."

Carter finished the meal and called Washington. Yvonne was close. She had traced the fund transfers to a Swiss "other" bank. Now all they needed was paper proof that the receiving account was General Tebessa's private party. She was hard at work finding a pigeon in the bank who could be broiled into cooperating.

Carter told her his southern France location for the next few days and hung up.

"Ismael . . ."

The little man appeared out of nowhere without a sound. *"Oui, monsieur?"*

"I'm leaving for Nice this evening. Watch her while I'm gone, but don't interfere."

"I understand, monsieur."

"And I'll need a tailor, someone who works fast and can make me look like a playboy oil executive with dollars to burn or spend."

The brown face broke into a wide smile. "I have a brother . . ."

"I figured you did."

"Monsieur Cologne?"

"Yes, Serge, go ahead."

"A woman has moved into his villa. We have not been able to get an identity on her yet."

"And our man?"

"He spent the afternoon shopping. He ordered four suits from a local tailor earlier, and picked them up about an hour ago. I followed him to the airport and learned that he has chartered a plane to Nice.''

"I will have our people pick him up there," Cologne
replied. "I have reports that Washington and London are
tracing all our large cash movements. They must guess something.''

"There is a commercial flight to Nice in an hour,"
Bowldor replied.

"Take it, but make no move for him yet. If this man from
Casablanca is dangerous, we will see what he is up to before
taking any action.''

"Very good, Mönsieur Cologne."

Carter dressed very carefully in a white dinner jacket, a
white-on-white shirt, and dark trousers. He left his suite in
the Hôtel de Paris at exactly ten and walked across the square
to the casino.

Inside, he paid two thousand francs for access to the upper
floor and took the seat that had been reserved for him at the
chemin de fer table. There were six other players at the table.
The seat beside his was empty.

From the hotel, he had already established his credit at two
hundred thousand francs. He guessed that anyone in the
know would tip off Angela Picard.

He was right. A half hour later a tall, statuesque woman
with white-blond hair and aristocratic features claimed the
empty chair.

"Good evening, Madame Picard," the croupier said with
a bow.

"Good evening, Pierre. Ten thousand, please."

Carter won and lost for the next hour, letting his boredom
show. The woman bet carefully, neither winning nor losing
great amounts. The Killmaster noticed that twice she won the
bank but passed it.

Angela Picard wasn't there to gamble. She was on a
hunting expedition.

When Carter bet an unusually large bank and lost, she
turned to him with sad eyes.

"Monsieur is not lucky tonight."

"It isn't my game."

"Oh?"

"No, I'm an American. I'd just as soon roll my sleeves up and get into an old-fashioned Texas poker game."

"Texas? You have ranches?"

"Sure do," Carter said, laughing. "Dogies on top and oil underneath! Can I buy you a drink, ma'am?"

"That would be most pleasant."

By two in the morning she had informed him that she knew of an expatriate American who also played poker.

"He has a yacht anchored in the harbor."

"Sounds like my kind of man!" Carter roared enthusiastically.

They had breakfast together at three in the morning, and Carter said good-night. But not before Angela Picard had promised to introduce him to her "friend" the following afternoon.

Robert Sievers repacked his briefcase with the work he had brought home from the previous night. Carter's plan was good, and by going over the procedure, Sievers had come up with all the help State could give him without the U.S. being implicated.

In the kitchen he gulped a cup of coffee, then headed for the front door.

"Oh, darling, must you always leave so early?"

His petite blond wife of six months, Melissa, staggered sleepily from the bedroom.

"Sorry, sweetheart, but I've got a project on."

"We never have breakfast together," she pouted.

"Tomorrow, I promise." He brushed her lips with his own and stepped out onto the stoop.

"Come home early, darling. I'll make a roast and we'll stay in tonight."

"I'll try," he said over his shoulder, and bounced down the steps.

As he did every morning when in Washington, Sievers turned right, walked two blocks, and turned right again. In the middle of the block he darted into Carl's News and Cigars.

The place was empty other than Carl himself and a jeans-and-sweat-shirt waif gorging on romance novels near the rear of the store.

"Morning, Carl."

"Morning, Mr. Sievers. I have your papers and cigars right here."

"Thanks. I think I'll get an *International Herald* this morning as well."

"Very well, sir. They're on the back rack there with the foreign papers."

Robert Sievers had to turn sideways in the narrow aisle, as did the girl passing him.

"Excuse me."

"S'okay," she said with a smile, and moved to the front of the shop.

Sievers passed out of sight to the far rear rack. He plucked a *Herald* from the top of the rack and glanced over the headlines as he moved back to the counter.

He was so absorbed in the paper that he took no notice of the fear on the old tobacconist's face, nor did he notice that the young girl had moved behind the counter to stand just to the old man's side.

"Take it! Hell, it's all the cash in the place—I never open up with more than two hundred. Take it!"

Carl's stammered words brought Sievers up short. It was then that he saw the man's quivering hands pushing wads of bills across the counter. His eyes followed the path of the bills, directly to the long snout of a silenced pistol in the small blonde's hands.

Good God, Sievers thought, rooted to the spot, *I've walked right into the middle of a robbery*!

He was trying to think of an out, of some way to help Carl,

when he saw the old man stagger back against the racks of cigarettes, clutching his chest.

There was no sound, but Sievers knew that Carl had been shot. Blood stained half his shirt front and oozed through his splayed fingers as he slumped to the floor out of sight behind the counter.

Then the girl had turned to face Sievers.

"You shot him, for God's sake!" Sievers bellowed. "Why the hell did you shoot him, you nut? He was giving you the money! Why . . ."

Sievers never got an answer to his question.

The gun barked. The girl moved forward and fired again.

The second shot, in the center of Robert Sievers's forehead, wasn't actually needed. The first bullet, just left of the center of his chest, had already killed him.

The gun disappeared in the large bag hanging from the girl's shoulder. On top of it she shoveled in the money from the counter and rechecked the register.

It was cleaned out.

From the old man's wallet she extracted another forty dollars. From Sievers's she took two hundred. Both wallets were thrown randomly on the floor.

Her experienced eyes went through Sievers's briefcase in a matter of seconds. She extracted a manila file and three individual sheets. These were also stuffed into her shoulder bag.

A quick check of both men's throats made sure they were dead.

Unhurried, she set the cardboard clock on the front door sign: Be back in "1" hour.

She turned the sign outward, closed the door, and strolled away.

The call came just before lunch. Angela Picard practically gushed over the phone.

"It is just a little combination tea and cocktail party on the

Long Shot . . . isn't that just the most adorable name for a boat? The launch will begin ferrying guests out any time after two. Do come, Nicky darling, I am sure you will enjoy it!''

Carter winced as he hung up the phone. Already he was "Nicky darling.''

He waited until three before going down to the pier. By that time, he was pretty sure the salon and the decks of the *Long Shot* would be teeming with people and he could observe before being observed.

He was right. He stepped on deck, secured a drink, and melted into the crowd before Angela Picard had noticed he was aboard.

The crowd was about what he had expected. There were several of the vacationing American oilmen, a contingent of the usual jet-setters, and the usual amount of hangers-on, a sheik or two, and the prerequisite number of bosomy French film starlets.

The Killmaster had worked his way through most of the hors d'oeuvres buffet when Angela spotted him.

"Nicky darling, I am so happy you could make it!'' she gushed. "Come along and meet James!''

Rowland was a compact six feet, with an easy smile and a lot of rough edges that seemed to add to his charm. He had a cute blonde on his right arm and a left hand full of gin and tonic.

"Carter, always glad to meet another American in these weird places.''

He shook hands without removing his arm from the blonde, and the movement made the front of her dress dance.

"Rowland, nice boat,'' Carter nodded.

"Yeah, sometimes it's convenient when you want to get to cooler climes in a hurry.''

His one good eye behind yellow sunglasses didn't miss a trick. Carter had the uncomfortable feeling that the man had already sized him, but he had gone too far to back off now.

Angela had done her duty introducing them and already moved away.

"Angela tells me you didn't fare too well at the shimmy table last night."

"Frankly, no," Carter replied. "Foreign games don't do much for me, and I don't like playing against house percentages."

The grin was ear to ear. "You sound like a poker man!"

"Usually."

"We have a little friendly game down in the salon every night . . . nothing big, fifty grand buy-in. There's always an empty chair."

"I might take you up on it."

"Do, I think you'd enjoy it. We usually start around ten. By the way . . ."

"Yeah?"

"Angela said you were in oil."

"That's right . . . and you?"

A hearty laugh rumbled up from his barrel chest. "I used to be in the book business. I'm retired now."

Carter threw a look at the blonde. "It must be nice."

"It is. Ten?"

"I'll be there."

Carter moved away, feeling the man's eyes boring into his back. He had been nailed and he knew it. Rowland didn't make the kind of money he did as a gambler by not being able to size up a mark. He had already sized up Carter as anything but a mark. The Killmaster only hoped that Rowland just needed a player to legitimately round out the game. The chances were that the man who called himself Rollo already had his mark for the night.

Carter killed another hour, and slipped away.

A telex was waiting in his box at the hotel:

GOT IT, ALSO A COOPERATIVE PIGEON. YOUR PEOPLE SETTING IT UP IN ZURICH NOW. SHOULD GO DOWN IN A DAY OR TWO. AUDITOR NAME: ANTHONY ZOREZ.
YVONNE

Carter checked planes and connections, and made a reservation for Zürich for the following day.

He was about to strip down for a nap, when the phone jangled.

"Nick, it's Ginger."

"Yeah?"

"Bob Sievers was shot this morning."

"Jesus, a termination?"

"It's hard to say. He was an innocent bystander in a tobacco store holdup. Both Bob and the owner were killed."

"It smells."

"Maybe. Hawk says you should watch yourself. You know we can't put people on you from here without putting the agency in the middle."

"I know. Don't worry about it. I'm getting help from another quarter. Anything new from Yvonne?"

"She's setting up Zürich. She's good, Nick. I think we should keep her."

"I'd second that. You know where to reach me in Zürich."

"Yeah, talk to you. Wait a minute . . ." There was a long pause before her voice came back. "You're right, it smells. Bob was shot by a silenced nine-millimeter. They found both the shell casings. It was probably a Beretta."

Carter swallowed hard. "Okay, they want to play hardball, I'll accommodate 'em."

TEN

Henry Barth-Hayes looked, sounded, and carried himself exactly like what he was, a retired commander in the Queen's Royal Navy. He had a red-flecked-with-gray handlebar mustache, iron in his spine, and a ton of his wife's money on the table in front of him.

The cut for seating put Barth-Hayes directly to Carter's left.

To his right was Juan Sebastian from Argentina, a lot of beef and enough shares in oil to be a high roller no matter where he went in the world. He was dark all over . . . skin, expensive suit, tie, and mustache.

His stature was small and his hands sported long, delicate fingers like a woman's. But the ear-to-ear scar under his chin and the immobile, beadlike black eyes told Carter that Sebastian hadn't made his money from any silver spoon shoved in his mouth by his daddy.

Directly across from Carter sat Clinton Wilson. Rowland had mentioned that Wilson was a Kansas City boy into meat packing and Oklahoma oil. He looked the part, in alligator boots, string tie, and Stetson.

Wilson was to Rowland's left, and on his right sat Teddy Blaine III. Carter already knew the face from countless pictures in magazines and newspapers. Young Blaine had devoted the years since his father's death to spending the vast fortune the old man had pilfered from the stock market before the SEC stopped such things.

He carried himself with an air of amused boredom, and his dress added to the image: a lightweight white tropical suit, and a silk shirt with the top three buttons left open to show his hairy but narrow chest and the ton of gold decorating it.

It wasn't difficult to spot Rowland's pigeon for the night. He would give and take with the other four, but before the night was done, little Teddy would be down to his shorts.

Besides the six players, there was a steward in the room to supply fresh cards and drinks. At six-six and three hundred pounds, with a flat face and catchers' mitts for hands, he fooled no one except perhaps Blaine.

His name was Bogdan, and he was Rollo's muscle.

The salon's other occupant was a short blonde with a chest that defied gravity, and a face and eyes that defied existence; both were utterly vacant. She sat on one of the lounges away from the table reading a picture magazine. Carter guessed that if there were words instead of pictures, she would be reading it upside down.

"Gentlemen, we'll play English etiquette. Any comment on your hand or another player's forfeits the pot. Since we're all gentlemen here, I think we can agree that if the well runs dry, markers will be accepted."

There was a chorus of agreement, and each man cut for deal. Rowland won it and shuffled. He had short, thick fingers, but he played the cards like a virtuoso works the keys of a piano.

The game was Hold 'Em, with unlimited raises, no limit, and a hundred-dollar ante. It's a high roller's brand of poker, not for the squeamish, the man short of capital, or the amateur.

Two cards are dealt to each player after the ante. The betting goes around and then the flop is made, three cards face up in the center of the table. These cards, plus two more flipped one at a time after more betting, are community cards to be used by all the players.

This makes Hold 'Em a variation on Seven-Card Stud, with the difference being the five community cards. The other difference is that a lousy hand can be turned into a outright winner on the last card, costing the man who thought he had a big hand a bundle.

Sebastian and Wilson both showed the calm of the professional gambler, but not the skill. Henry Barth-Hayes played tight, scrutinizing every card, every bet, and every tic in another's eye. But with all that, he evidenced a nervousness that didn't fit with his supposed high-roller status.

From the beginning, Carter felt that the Englishman shouldn't be in the game.

Rowland was laid back. As the game rocked along, he suckered Carter once and Blaine several times with lead-in bluffs from supposedly pat hands, only to come back with the real thing when he had psyched the table just enough.

Carter got the feeling that he was waiting for something to happen, so the Killmaster did the same.

Three hours into the game, personal characteristics started to show. Most marked was Teddy Blaine. He was down about fifteen thousand, not much more than Sebastian, Wilson, and Carter himself, but he began to whine.

Blaine didn't like to lose, and the more he lost, the more the rest of the table heard about it. By the four-hour mark, Blaine had called for more inter-deal cuts and more between-hand fresh decks than Carter had ever seen in a high-stakes game.

Early on, Carter had tabbed Blaine as a bluffer. Skillful bluffing in Hold 'Em—Rowland's brand, for instance—can be an art. In young Teddy Blaine's case, it was a disease. Bluffing with him was like overdrinking or oversmoking; once the habit was acquired, it became damned near unbreakable.

Carter had a hunch that when the time came to break Blaine and send him on his way, Rowland would capitalize on that weakness.

When at last a break was called for a stretch and relaxation, it was apparent that Blaine was a bad-tempered, petulant child. He was proud of his poker-playing ability and didn't like to be bested.

He was also a drinker. High-stakes poker and alcohol don't mix.

Carter went to the head, washed his face, and ran into Rowland by the bar when he emerged.

"Drink, Carter?"

"Perrier, no ice."

He smiled and fixed two. The big muscle, Bogdan, was taking a high-powered bourbon and branch water to Blaine.

"Satisfied with the game?"

Carter shrugged. "Fairly tame so far. These the usual players?"

"Only Barth-Hayes is new. Teddy's played a couple of times. He brought the Englishman in tonight."

Carter adjusted his tie in the back-bar mirror and shot his cuffs. "Maybe the second round will get a little more lively."

"Let's hope so," Rowland replied.

Fifteen minutes later they returned to the table. They were barely seated when Blaine suggested they raise the ante to five hundred and waive the table stakes.

The Englishman looked even more uncomfortable, but no one objected. Carter caught an amused glint in Rowland's face.

The tide in the game changed at once. The chips in front of Sebastian, Wilson, and Carter began to dwindle. The piles in front of the now smiling Blaine and the nervous Englishman grew alarmingly.

Rowland played tight, neither winning nor losing.

Then Carter realized why.

Blaine was a cheater, a thief in big-time poker parlance. And he had an ally in the Englishman Barth-Hayes.

Chances were good that Rowland knew it but was waiting for the right hand and the right time, not to expose Blaine, but to break him.

If a Hold 'Em player is sharp enough, rich enough, and has the guts, he can take a thief every time.

All Rowland was doing was waiting for the two thieves to fleece everyone else before he fleeced them.

Carter started playing tight himself and watching hands. Then he spotted it: a palmed card, a queen, by Blaine when he put the deck together for the commander's deal. That pot, a small one, was won by Wilson.

Then it was Blaine's deal. A queen came up in the flop and Barth-Hayes bet in, building the pot for Blaine. Carter and Rowland dived out, but the others were suckered in for the kill. Before the turn of the last card, Barth-Hayes bowed out and Blaine raked in close to a forty-grand pot.

He immediately called for a new deck, and Carter spotted the corner of a ten under Blaine's shiny Gucci toe. It had been the down card he'd replaced with the queen in his last hand.

If they were running true to form, it would be Barth-Hayes's turn. Sure enough, the Englishman reached for the cards, shoving them together for Rowland's deal. This time Carter helped him. He'd been working toward an ace, but Carter maneuvered an eight under his hand and he had to be satisfied with that.

Carter drew a ten-king down and bet like a wild man. Another ten, a nine, and an eight came up in the flop. Just as before, Blaine started betting in, building the pot before dropping out to supposedly let the Englishman rake it in.

During this, Carter spilled the cigarettes from his case and, while retrieving them, gently rescued the ten from under Blaine's foot. He tore the corner from the ten and slipped the rest of the card in his pocket.

With the addition of the last card in the center, it held a ten, nine, deuce, and a pair of eights. That would give Barth-Hayes three eights and Carter absolutely nothing with his king and ten in the hole.

The betting got heavy, head to head. Then Carter slipped the torn edge of the ten into his hand, covering the king. While he pushed in his biggest raise of the night, he "accidentally'' opened his hand to Barth-Hayes's watchful eye.

Where the Englishman's skin had been a light tan, it suddenly grew colorless. He was facing a triple-ten hand and an eight-thousand-dollar raise against his three eights.

He promptly folded, and Carter raked in the pot. It was his deal, and this time he called for a new deck. If that wasn't enough to give Barth-Hayes and Blaine the picture, Carter, while dealing, dropped the torn corner of the ten in the Englishman's lap.

Barth-Hayes had another complexion change and started sending signals across the table to young Blaine.

Out of the corner of his eye, Carter could see that Rowland had spotted it all, and from the new tight-lipped look in his face, his host didn't like it.

Rowland had wanted the cheating to continue until the two roosters were nice and fat with everyone else's coin for plucking.

Carter was floored when Blaine ignored the danger. Instead of halting the cheating, he just changed the method.

This time Carter backed off and let it happen. Four big hands later, Sebastian and Wilson were forced out of the game. Between them, they had lost a quarter of a million.

High-stakes poker is just what the name implies.

Blaine was ripe, and both Rowland and Carter knew it. Now it was only a matter of who did the plucking.

It was Carter's deal. "Thousand-a-hand ante?"

Blaine was sweating. "Sure."

Rowland nodded.

Barth-Hayes looked as if he were about to faint.

The cards went out. Rowland and the Englishman passed. Blaine smirked and bet five thousand.

It was odds-on he had a pair wired, probably high, if he was sticking to his style.

Carter checked his hole cards: two tens wired. He lashed the pot with a ten-thousand raise.

Rowland looked as if he would chew the table apart, or rip

Carter in two with his bare hands. He'd already gotten the picture, and he didn't like it.

His pigeon was slipping away.

He called the ten grand.

The Englishman groaned and threw in.

Carter dealt the flop. It showed an ace, four, ten.

Blaine smiled and bet fifty thousand. Carter saw that, and raised twenty-five.

Rowland's face sagged. He was beaten and he knew it. Like a wise man, he threw in to wait for another day.

Blaine raised again, and Carter called.

He flipped the fourth card in the flop. It was a four, giving Blaine a full house, aces over fours.

He almost peed his pants.

He bet it, and Carter raised him. It was a long shot and the Killmaster knew it. But he had to take it. It might take hours for Blaine to hold another hand strong enough to make him bet his ass.

"Would you like to call, Mr. Blaine?" Rowland said, calmly lighting a short cigar.

"I'm thinking, goddamnit, I'm thinking!"

At last he called and raised again, using every chip in front of him.

Carter reraised.

Blaine's shirt was soaked through now and clinging to his skin. Where the shirt wasn't, his chest was glistening.

"I'll have to play light. You said you'd take markers."

Carter looked to his left. "*Mr. Rowland* said he would take markers."

Rowland looked at the overhead and blew smoke rings.

"What the hell, I'm good for it," Blaine whined. "Jesus Christ, I can buy or sell either one of you!"

Rowland's hand came down on the table like a rifle shot. "Easy, son. First thing you know, you'll have the hair in my ass curlin', and that does funny things to my temper."

Carter jumped in. "I'm sure your friend the commander

there would stand you with his pile. Wouldn't you do that, Mr. Barth-Hayes?''

"Yes, yes, of course." The Englishman pushed his stacks toward Teddy Blaine as though they were on fire.

The younger man accepted them without a word and counted out the call. His eyes watered as he looked at the remaining pile in front of him.

It was about forty thousand.

He pushed it in.

Carter matched it, and flipped the last card.

It was the fourth ten.

An audible gasp went around the table from everyone except the combatants. There was a second sharp intake of air when Carter pushed all his chips in.

Teddy Blaine chewed his upper lip so hard that tiny flecks of blood appeared on the pink skin. Carter could read his thoughts; they rolled across the table like vibrations from well-struck timpani.

Is that a fourth ten? Impossible. He's bluffing. I got a pat full house staring at me. He's got a full house, too, three fours over two tens. My three aces over fours beats him!

"I'll call."

"Light?" Carter said.

"Yeah, yeah, light."

Carter made some quick calculations in his head. "That will put you about eighty thousand light. Rowland?"

"I'll take the marker."

Carter turned over his wired tens.

Teddy's face turned pale and he slumped in his chair. "Shit."

"Another hand?" Carter said. "Or is that it for the evening?"

"If you gentlemen will excuse me," Barth-Hayes gasped, "I believe I've had enough." His face looked a little green as he headed for the hatch.

Blaine was boiling. His face was red and his whole body was quivering in his chair.

"I didn't know you were going to let cardsharks into the game, Rollo!"

Rowland smiled. "Neither did I."

"I'll tell you this, you bastard," the kid went on, not realizing the tenseness that had entered Rowland's body, "you'll never get another fucking game around here!"

"Listen, you little—"

Carter quickly put his arms between them. "Gentlemen, gentlemen, we're all sporting people here. Mr. Blaine, you lead me to believe that you think you've been taken."

"You bet your ass I have!"

Carter flicked his eyes to Rowland's eye behind the yellow glasses, and got a quizzical stare in return.

"Then I propose a sporting wager to settle the question. I'd say there is about a half million of my money on the table there. Would you agree?"

" 'Bout that," Blaine said warily.

"And that gold gracing your neck . . . I'd say that was worth about fifty grand."

Blaine shrugged. "Give or take."

"Fine." Carter shuffled the cards and set the squared deck in the center of the table. "Then I'd like to make a wager . . . my table against your gold."

"Name it."

"I'll wager," Carter said, turning his attention to Rowland, "that our host can touch his eye to that deck without moving his head from where it presently is."

Carter could see Rowland biting the inside of his lip to keep from laughing.

"You're on!" Blaine said, yanking the gold from around his neck and dumping it on the table.

Calmly Rowland took off his glasses, popped his eye from its socket, and set it on the deck of cards.

"Bastards!" Blaine screeched, leaping to his feet, all reason gone from his head now.

"Hell, son," Rowland said calmly, "I'll bet my boat against your butt I can do it with the other eye."

Teddy Blaine grabbed the vapid blonde's hand and rushed from the salon.

Rowland turned to face Carter. "Boy done completely lost his sense of reason."

"It would appear so."

"Get you a drink?"

"Much obliged," Carter replied, "just as soon as you cash these into real spending money."

They were in the bow, a brandy bottle between them and a briefcase fully packed with cash in front of them.

"I should have known you'd spot 'em," Rowland said.

"You've seen them do it before?"

"Yeah, about a month ago in Las Palmas. I've been waiting a long time to set that up, Carter. You took us all."

"When were you going to move?"

"Just about the time you did, maybe the next hand." Rowland had been inspecting the stars. Now he turned to face Carter. "I know just about every big-time shooter on both sides of the Atlantic. You got smarts and class, but you're not one of 'em."

"No, I'm not."

"And I don't think you knew about Teddy and the commander before the game started."

"No, I didn't. But I knew you had a pigeon."

"Then, partner, just who the hell are you?"

"I'm a man who needs a job of moving done, and I think you're the man who can do the moving."

"What, and from where to where?"

Carter spread the map. "Here to here. Arms. The big stuff you get at sea. The little stuff you load somewhere in the western Sahara. I gather you know a friendly ship captain?"

"I know one. How much?"

Carter nodded toward the briefcase. "That, minus the gold, for a down payment. The receiver matches it on delivery."

Rowland roared. "You're payin' me with my own money!"

"But I'm doubling it," Carter replied, smiling. "Do we have a deal?"

"Mister, I don't know who you are. But then I don't much give a damn. When?"

"About two weeks' time, if all goes well. Get your ship a few days before then, and cruise Cape St. Vincent off Portugal. Here's a number in Casablanca where you can always reach me. I already know the *Long Shot*'s frequency and private call letters."

Rowland reached forward and snapped the lid on the briefcase. "How do you know I'll perform?"

"Because a gambler can't go back on his word. If he did, where would he get his markers cashed when he went broke?"

"I'll see you in Morocco, my man."

ELEVEN

Carter taxied from Kloten Airport into downtown Zürich. During the fifteen-minute ride he thumbed through a brochure a young girl had thrust into his hand while he was waiting for his baggage.

He could care less about the Giacometti collection in the art museum, or the Eastern antiquities on display at the Reitberg.

But one thing did catch his eye: the Olympiad swimming pool. It would be a perfect place to arrange his meet with Anthony Zorez.

"He's a gambler, and in over his head," Ginger Bateman had told him over the phone that morning between planes in the Frankfurt airport. "Our Zürich man will give you the particulars when you arrive."

"How deep is he in?" Carter had asked.

"Farther down than he can ever get out. Yvonne got the word from a couple of London execs after she pressured them. He's already done the deed a couple of times, so he's prime."

The cab rolled past the lake and into the Bahnhofstrasse, the street of gold. Even from the street, Carter could see the second-floor windows gleam. Displayed alongside the banks' foreign exchange rates and late stock prices were trays and trays of bullion bars and shining coins.

He spotted the plaque of the bank he wanted and leaned forward in the seat. "This will be fine. Stop here, please."

He paid the driver and entered the bank. A porter checked his name against the list of appointments, and a second man ushered him upstairs into the inner sanctum.

"Herr Carter, it is a pleasure to meet you."

"Herr Knowles."

Frederich Knowles was the solid burgher type, the kind of man other men immediately trust. This trait is most important in a Swiss banker.

Carter seated himself in front of the huge desk. After the usual ritual of coffee and small talk, the two men got down to business.

The Killmaster opened his briefcase and withdrew several pages which he passed to Knowles.

"Here are the letters of incorporation on Togland Limited."

The banker perused the papers and allowed himself a brief smile.

Togland had been incorporated in Liechtenstein the day before. Its main assets would be deposited in Knowles's bank now. Anyone attempting to trace the actual ownership of Togland, Ltd., or the company's source of funds, would come up against a stone wall in two places.

"I trust everything is in order?" Carter asked.

"Most definitely."

Carter handed across another paper. "Here is the authorization of my transfer of funds from my Bahamian bank, one million dollars."

"It will be deposited at once."

The account in the Bahamas was an AXE blind. It fed money to several projects around the world. In this case, the one million would only serve as seed money. Much more would be needed for the Togo project.

"In the next few days a great deal more will be deposited in the account. The instructions for its dispersal when the time comes will be sent personally to you by telex."

"I understand completely," Knowles said, nodding.
"The papers will be ready within the hour. If you would care
to wait . . ."

"No," Carter replied, "I have another appointment. I'll
pick them up in the morning."

"Excellent."

Good-byes were said, and Carter hit the street. He walked
the short distance to the Carlton Elite and checked in. A
single envelope was waiting for him.

In his room, he opened it and dialed the number it contained.

"Shipman's Rare Clocks."

"Good morning. I'm interested in a rare timepiece, the
Loudain. I understand there were only a few of them made,
around the turn of the century."

"That is quite true, sir . . . forty-three to be exact."

"Do you have access to such a clock?"

"We do, sir. But such a transaction would be very expensive. Perhaps it would be best to meet in person to discuss
it."

"Fine. Where would you suggest?" Carter asked.

"Shall we say the Grill Room in the Baur au Lac in a half
hour? They have an excellent lunch."

"I'll see you then."

Carter hung up and changed his shirt and tie. In the lobby,
he deposited the briefcase containing Teddy Blaine's gold in
a hotel safe-deposit box, then cabbed to the Baur au Lac.

The Grill Room was crowded with early arrivals for lunch.
Carter found Rudolph Fitzmeyer at a secluded table on the
terrace. He was nursing a glass of white wine and checking
the room from behind thick glasses.

Fitzmeyer was a Swiss citizen, but he didn't completely
believe in the total neutrality doctrine. He had been working
for American intelligence for the last twenty years. His
export clock shop on the Bahnhofstrasse made a perfect cover
for AXE's man in Zürich.

"Rudy."

"Nicholas."

The old man didn't rise. He merely nodded and motioned Carter to a chair. Carter seated himself and ordered a scotch from the waiter.

There was no conversation between the two men until the drink had been delivered and the waiter had left.

"I trust the papers were in order?"

"Of course," Carter replied, nodding. "You've always been a very thorough man. Togland is on-line to be used when we find our seller."

The old man passed an envelope to Carter. "Evidently that has been achieved. This came in the pouch this morning."

Carter pocketed it. "I'll check it later. What's the latest on Anthony Zorez?"

"The young man is very scared. Evidently he was almost caught the last time he breached Swiss bank security and tattletaled secrets."

"But he will cooperate?"

Fitzmeyer nodded. "The amount of your offer has assuaged his fears."

"He has the material?"

"He claims he will have it by noon tomorrow."

Carter made his suggestion of a lunchtime swim at the outdoor pool, and chose two o'clock as the time.

"I will pass it along, as well as your description. Here is a photograph of Zorez."

Carter slipped the picture into his pocket along with the envelope.

They ordered, and dined in silence. Over coffee and brandy, the conversation resumed.

"You have been able to contact Goulanda?"

"Yes," the old man replied. "Needless to say, going through two intermediaries was very difficult, but he has agreed to the meeting. He will fly into Geneva secretly tomorrow evening."

"And I will meet him . . . ?"

"In Coppet. I have arranged for the Château du Mer to be at the president's disposal for the night. He has also agreed to bring only his general and one aide."

"But he has no hint of our source?"

"None."

Carter stood. "I'll be in touch."

Fitzmeyer's face cracked in a wan smile of dismissal. He had seen and done all of this before, many times. And he would do it many more times.

Carter bypassed the taxi stand and walked back to his own hotel. Several times he took small detours. The people tailing him were good. In fact they were excellent; he couldn't pinpoint a single one of them.

But he knew they were there.

Back in his room at the Carlton, he consulted the paper given him by Mock and dialed.

A woman's voice answered in German. "Four-four-six-one."

"Alpine, this is Drumbeat."

"One moment."

Carter could hear the call being switched to another line, and then a deep bass voice came on, speaking heavily accented English. "This is Alpine. What can I do for you?"

"I've had a tail for the last two days. Are they yours?"

"Not directly. We've kept track of you, of course, but only within the cities, not between. You've had one man on you all the way. He picked up two more at Kloten when you landed. They've watched you all day while we've watched them."

Carter thought for a moment, then made his decision. Obviously they had zeroed in on him. It was time to let them know that he knew, and do a little payback for Bob Sievers.

"I have another meeting tomorrow afternoon and tomorrow evening. It's important that they don't know with whom. I want them out."

"We'll ring you back in an hour."

Carter replaced the receiver and moved to the balcony. He lit a cigarette and pried open the envelope that Fitzmeyer had given him.

There were six sheets, all neatly typed in single space.

The first two were an update on Togo and Cyclops. Since the coup, the conglomerate's offices throughout the world had been on the move. Most were already shut down, and telex codes were already being changed.

New base of operations: Togo.

World Bank had already gone into the country and performed an audit. Everything was on the up and up, but reports were that the banks in Lomé had grown very rich almost overnight from tremendous infusions of new capital.

Also, while all other industry and trade had remained nationalized, the banks had reverted to private ownership.

Listed as the banks' board chairman was one Sir Howard Doyle.

There was little doubt of it now. Cyclops had moved in to control the country.

The third sheet was a personal memo from Yvonne, approved and countersigned by Ginger Bateman.

TO: CARTER

FROM: MOLINA

AS YOU CAN SEE, ALL SUPPOSITIONS ON TOGO COUP RE: CYCLOPS PROVING OUT. HEADS OF VARIOUS CYCLOPS DIVISIONS IN WEST GERMANY, NETHERLANDS, U.S.A., FRANCE, AND ENGLAND HAVE ALREADY DECLARED CORPORATE MOVES TO TOGO.

CYCLOPS VESSELS, APPROXIMATELY 127, ALREADY REREGISTERED TOGO. NEW HEAD OF TOGO MARITIME COMMISSION, ONE LARS GUSTAFSSON. GUSTAFSSON ALSO ON INTERNATIONAL BOARD OF CYCLOPS.

HOPE ZÜRICH CONTACT, ZOREZ, CAN AFFIRM FINANCES WITH PROOF AND ALSO TIE-IN PROBABLY PAYOFF TO TEBESSA.

SUBJECT: SUPPLIER
        COMPANY NAME: CHADRON

TELEX: CHA BRAX

SOLE STOCKHOLDER: CHANDRA BRAXTON

DOSSIER ON BRAXTON AND RESUMÉ OF COMPANY HOLDINGS, WORTH, AND OUR OPPORTUNITIES ATTACHED.

PERSONAL EVALUATION TAGGED.

      MUCH LUCK,
      Y.M.

Carter read and reread the winding, involved tale of Chandra Braxton.

CHANDRA BRAXTON, BORN BA' ESTEL, BEIRUT, 1940, JEWISH MOTHER, LEBANESE FATHER. EDUCATED FRANCE AND SWITZERLAND. FATHER AND MOTHER BOTH KILLED WHILE HELPING SYRIAN JEWS ESCAPE TO ISRAEL. 1964, MET AND MARRIED FRENCH MUNITIONS MANUFACTURER, DAMIEN BRAXTON, TWENTY YEARS HER SENIOR. WHEN THE U.S., BRITAIN AND FRANCE IMPOSED ARMS EMBARGO, MADAME BRAXTON FORMED AN ANTILLES COMPANY FOR THE LEGAL PURPOSE OF IMPORTING ARMS FROM HER HUSBAND'S COMPANY. IT WAS NEVER PROVEN—BUT WIDELY SUSPECTED AND GENERALLY OVERLOOKED—THAT HER COMPANY SUPPLIED MASSIVE ARMS TO ISRAEL DURING THE EMBARGO AND PRIOR TO THE SIX-DAY WAR.

MADAME BRAXTON BECAME WEALTHY IN HER OWN RIGHT. SHE TOOK OVER ALL OF HER HUSBAND'S HOLDINGS WHEN HE DIED IN 1975. WHAT HAD ONCE BEEN PROFITABLE BUSINESS SOON BECAME A BOOMING, MULTIMILLION-DOLLAR ENTERPRISE.

IN THE TRADE, IT IS GENERALLY BELIEVED THAT MADAME BRAXTON HAS POWERFUL BACKING AND PRIVATE AGREEMENTS WITH BOTH THE FINANCIAL POWERS AND THE INTELLIGENCE COMMUNITIES OF SEVERAL COUNTRIES. EVEN LEGITIMATE ARMS AUCTIONS HAVE BEEN WON BY BRAXTON AGENTS WITH RIGGED BIDS. IN SEVERAL CASES, COLLUSION WITH OFFICIALS OF THE SELLING COUNTRIES HAS BEEN SUSPECTED BUT NEVER PROVED.

NOTE: NICK, CHADRON IS BASICALLY ON THE UP AND UP, ALBEIT A LITTLE SHADY. OF ALL THE COMPANIES I CAME UP WITH, ONLY THIS ONE HAS THE WHEREWITHAL-AS WELL AS THE EXPERTISE-TO PULL OFF THE KIND OF OPERATION WE NEED AND KEEP IT HIDDEN.

CHANDRA BRAXTON RARELY TRAVELS. SHE HAS AN ESTATE ON MYKONOS OFF THE GREEK COAST, AND RARELY LEAVES IT.

FRANK LAYTON, OUR AMBASSADOR TO GREECE, CAN GET YOU IN. FROM THERE, YOU'RE ON YOUR OWN.

Carter read all six sheets a third and a fourth time, then touched his lighter to them.

Yvonne had done her job with her computers; now it was up to him.

By late the next evening, if all went well, the operation would be completely set up.

All he needed then was the arms, and a supplier that could hide their purchase, their sale, and their destination.

Chandra Braxton looked as if she and her Chadron Company fit the bill perfectly.

By the time the ashes had curled to dust, the phone was ringing again.

"Yes?"

"Alpine here. At midnight, leave your hotel. Walk to the Grossmunster Cathedral. In the north side parking lot, there will be a red Fiat, license number F292-449. The keys are in the ashtray. Do you have that, Drumbeat?"

"Got it."

"Drive around the lake and take the N-1 north to St. Gallen. Seven miles short of St. Gallen, take the Arnriswil road due north toward Bodensee. You will see Alpine Road 336 to your right. Take it to the scenic view and wait."

"I've got it."

"And be very careful, mein Herr. Alpine 336 is a very narrow, treacherous road. Accidents are extremely frequent."

Carter hung up and left the hotel. He walked to the American consulate on Zollikerstrasse and used his clearance for access to the code room.

He acknowledged receipt to Dupont Circle and Yvonne for the material, and prepared a second message to Frank Layton in Athens requesting assistance and giving his ETA three days hence.

Back in his hotel, he loudly asked for an eleven o'clock wake-up call at the desk and retired to his room for a nap until then.

"Monsieur Cologne?"

"Yes, Serge, where are you?"

"In Zürich, monsieur. I am still with him. He is at the Carlton, and he has already met with one man."

"Marga is here, Serge. He is definitely an agent. His affiliation, other than the State Department, we do not know. Under what name is he registered?"

"Nicholas Paulson."

"His real name is Carter, and he was working with Sievers on a Togo connection. Our guess here is that they plan to somehow come to Goulanda's aid. It would be helpful if we know who he contacts in the next few days."

"Then you want him left alone to continue?"

"Yes, Serge, until he leads us to their key people. Neither the United States nor the United Kingdom will openly interfere. They must be searching for intermediaries. We want to know who they are."

"*Oui, monsieur. Au revoir.*"

"Serge, give me your full report when he arrives at his next stop. *Au revoir.*"

Carter smiled with grim satisfaction as he turned onto Alpine 336 and switched on the windshield wipers. The rain would make the job much easier for Mock's men.

The road was exactly as the man on the phone had described. It wound like a demented snake and climbed steadily upward. Now and then he passed a tavern or a small inn plastered to the side of the mountain, but other than that there was little sign of life and practically no traffic on the road.

Less than five miles out of Zürich he had spotted the tail, a dark green Cortina. Once they had reached the more desolate section of the N-l, the Cortina had dropped far back and Carter hadn't seen it since.

But he knew it was there, somewhere.

A half hour later he ran out of road into a large turn-around. He stopped and killed the engine and the lights.

Only then did he notice a black Citroën near the rail on the far side.

He stepped from the car, moved to the front, and sat on the fender.

The Citroën's lights blinked once. Carter put a cigarette between his lips and lit it, letting the flame from the lighter play for several seconds over his face.

The Citroën's engine purred to life and the car slid forward. It stopped right by Carter's knee, and the electric window slid down with a whirring smoothness.

The face beyond the window in the eerie glow was like a hundred others he had seen: wide, coarse, and typically Slavic, with a heavy nose and thin, grim lips.

"A dark green Cortina. I would like some documentation."

The window slid up and the car glided away down the mountain.

Carter walked across the turn-around to the rail. Three thousand feet below, he could see the twinkling lights of a village. He flipped his cigarette as far out as he could and watched the tiny red ash fall. It never hit the ground; it just diminished.

A half hour later he heard an explosion, and far to his left and below he saw a ball of flame rise in the night sky.

He lit another cigarette. It was down to the filter when he heard the purr of the Citroën enter the turn-around. When the car stopped behind him, he turned.

The window glided down and a hand emerged. In it were two passports and a small notebook.

Carter took them, the window slid up, and the Citroën was gone.

He examined the passports by the dashboard lights of the Fiat.

They were both French, one issued to Pascal Boyne, age twenty-seven, Marseille. The other had belonged to Serge Bowldor, age forty-three, Cannes.

Carter made a mental note of both addresses, and checked the notebook.

It was a travelogue on him for the past three days.

At the bottom of the mountain he dialed the clock shop.

"We are closed. If you will leave your number at the sound of the tone, I will return your call during regular business hours . . ."

Silence, and then the dull tone.

"Pick up, Fitzmeyer, it's me."

"Yes, Nicholas."

"I'm coming in. I want you to get something delivered for me as quickly as possible."

"The back door of the shop will be unlocked."

With no traffic, it took Carter less than two hours to get back to Zürich and the Bahnhofstrasse.

Killing his lights, he pulled into the alley parallel to the main street and parked. Two doors down, he let himself into the rear entrance of the clock shop.

Fitzmeyer was waiting for him in a robe, drinking coffee.

"Zorez has agreed to meet you. But he insists that the delivery of your goods and his must be made right there at the pool."

"That will be no problem. We can do it with locker keys." Carter handed him the passports and the notebook. "Burn the notebook and arrange for the passports to be quietly delivered to the Cyclops offices in Paris."

"No problem."

"Also, run a check on the names and addresses. I doubt if you can find any gainful means of employment, but it would help."

"I'll leave the information at the hotel."

"Good. Good-bye until next time, Rudy."

"Until then, Nicholas."

Carter left the Fiat where he had found it and returned to the Carlton.

From his room he called the villa in Casablanca. A very sleepy voice answered.

"Hi, having a wonderful time. Wish you were here."

"I can be," Leila said through a yawn. "Just tell me where you are."

"I won't be here that long. Did a character named Rowland get in touch?"

"Yes. He has a ship, The *Wayfarer Belle*, out of Tunis."

"Good. Tell him I'll be in touch by the end of the week.
Can you meet me in three days, Friday, at the Hilton in
Athens?"

"I'm at your disposal, remember?" she replied with a
chuckle.

"Yeah, 'til then."

Carter hung up and fell across the bed without undressing.

TWELVE

Carter, briefcase in hand, took the trolley to the Allmend Station. Behind him, Zürich gleamed like a clean, well-polished jewel against its green Alpine backdrop.

To the right of the station, through a thick forest, lay the Dolder Schwimmbad. The pool, its squat buildings, and the manicured lawns surrounding it were carved right into the side of the mountain.

Off the trolley and into the lane, the Killmaster followed laughing children and bored nannies. Five minutes later they emerged from the trees to find the Schwimmbad sparkling just below them in the afternoon sun.

Carter kept his pace close to a shuffle, staying well away from the crowd as he moved down to the pool's entrance. He knew that from high above, from somewhere on the superstructure's upper decks, he was being observed by Anthony Zorez.

Before leaving his hotel that morning, he had memorized the other man's face and then burned the photograph.

Now there was only one question remaining: would Zorez come through, or would fear of discovery make him back off at the last minute?

Bank and corporate security isn't taken lightly among the moneymen of Switzerland. Secrecy is the cornerstone of their livelihood; any breach of it can mean a lengthy jail sentence for the perpetrator. If there was a slipup and the bank officials somehow discovered what Zorez was doing, the man could find himself in a great deal of trouble.

The Killmaster paid his twenty francs admission fee and added five more for a private locker. When he reached it he stripped and pulled on the swim trunks and loose shirt he had purchased that morning in the hotel shop.

Before going out to the pool, he unlocked the briefcase and slid it carefully into the upper shelf of the locker.

When he walked back into the glaring sunshine, the wave-making machine was high in its hourly cycle. Hordes of children and a few oldsters were riding the machine-made waves or lolling on the simulated beach that made up two sides of the pool.

A large, grassy, gently sloping lawn took up the opposite side of the pool. He couldn't spot his man in or around the pool, so Carter opted for the lawn.

"Two, please."

An attendant set up two lounges with a small table between them. Carter ordered a light lunch with beer and told the boy he would order for his friend later.

For the next half hour he ate and girl-watched. When the food was gone and it was well past three, Carter started getting nervous.

He was about to find a phone and call Fitzmeyer, when he saw him: tall, with dark hair, Latin features, and a pencil-thin mustache.

He was lounging against the door leading to the lockers in such a way that he could scan the pool and the lawn where Carter sat. A cigarette bobbed in the corner of his mouth as he made calculated sweeps of the area with his dark eyes.

It was on one of those sweeps that Carter's own eyes caught his and held. Casually the Killmaster rolled the beer bottle to its side and turned his empty glass upside down beside it.

Anthony Zorez nodded.

Carter nodded back, and the man moved toward him. He was desperately trying for an air of casualness, but the tenseness in his body and the nervousness in his darting eyes were all too apparent.

Beside the lounge, he made one more sweep of the pool and then let his eyes settle on Carter.

"Is this chaise taken?"

"Yes, I'm meeting my banker."

Zorez grabbed the folded towel from the foot of the chaise, spread it, and stretched out. The hand holding a lit cigarette to a fresh one was shaking.

"This is very dangerous for me," he said through the cloud of smoke, looking at everyone but Carter.

"Yes, but I understand you have a good deal of experience at it." Carter, too, held his eyes to the front rather than meet those of Zorez.

"I have a family, a child. I could lose my position or be jailed or, worse yet, be deported."

"Frankly, Zorez, I don't give a damn and I don't want to haggle."

"I only want to—"

"I don't give a damn what you want."

The Killmaster moved his arm to the side and dropped the locker key with a clatter to the glass-topped table.

"Inspect the goods. If you don't like what you see, don't play."

"It is in gold?"

"That's right—nontraceable."

Zorez snatched the key and unwound from the lounge. Carter followed his walk to the locker room door, then cased the other bathers. No one was paying an iota of attention.

He was back in five minutes and set Carter's locker key as well as his own on the table.

"It is satisfactory."

"I figured it would be."

Carter took the keys and ambled from the lawn. Luckily, Zorez's locker was in the same row as his, four away.

He opened it, and then the briefcase inside. Taking a full ten minutes, he checked every document.

It was all there. A phony shell company for Tebessa to launder funds, a full accounting of cash in the dictator's accounts, and the sources of that cash.

All the new state documents were also there for the establishment of Cyclops's new Togo empire.

It was dynamite.

He waited until two small boys had changed and left before he switched the briefcases.

By the time he got back to the lawn, Zorez was sweating like a pig.

"You took long enough."

"I had more to examine than you did," Carter drawled, and dropped the other man's key on the table. "It was nice doing business with you. Have a nice day."

Zorez almost sprinted to the locker room.

"Bastard! Son of a whore! Bastard!"

Marcus Cologne clutched the two passports and fumed. He paced back and forth in front of the woman, his face growing more florid with each step.

"One thing is for sure," Marga Lund said quietly. "He knows about Cyclops."

"Or guesses. Whoever this Carter is, he is a daring and foolhardy man. He must be stopped!"

"I must find him first."

Cologne stopped directly in front of her chair. "He will be found, my dear. I doubt if he will stay in Zürich long, but wherever he surfaces, our people will spot him. And when they do, Marga, I want him taken out!"

Marga Lund smiled and shivered. "What kind of an accident, Marcus?"

"No accident," he hissed. "I want this one like the old

days, a rub out. He has sent us a warning, and I will return the favor to his people. And, Marga . . ."

"Yes, Marcus?"

"Make it especially messy, and very, very painful."

Marga Lund's eyes misted. She smiled and began to rub her thighs together.

Coppet was the preserve of the wealthy just outside Geneva. Winding lanes moved through large estates on rolling, heavily timbered acres. It was quiet, sedate, and as Carter drove the rental car slowly along, searching, he hoped it would stay exactly that way.

Château du Mer was no different from the plush manor houses surrounding it. It sat in a forested glen behind high brick walls and two enormous iron gates.

The Killmaster announced himself on the gate-to-house intercom, not with his name, but with the code designation Fitzmeyer had used to set up the meet in his first contact with Goulanda: "the connection."

A gravelly voice using Sandhurst English replied, and the Killmaster almost made the mistake of answering back in the same language. Instead he used a heavily accented French. His nationality, from the accent, could be anything.

The voice on the intercom switched to French at once and the gates swung open.

Carter followed the curt instructions and dropped the car into gear. He drove through, halted, and killed the engine and the lights. He had barely stepped from the car when a small but powerful-looking black man dressed in dark turtleneck, trousers, and sneakers appeared from the heavy shrubbery lining the drive.

A Beretta fit neatly in the palm of his right hand, and it didn't waver from Carter's gut as he moved forward.

"You are armed?"

"I am."

"On the hood of the car, please."

Carter unleathered Wilhelmina, placed the Luger on the hood, and did the same with Hugo. Then, without being asked, he turned his back on the man and assumed the position with his hands on the fender and his feet spread wide apart.

The Luger and Hugo disappeared under the turtleneck, and the man moved in behind Carter, putting the business end of the Beretta behind his right ear.

The frisk was quick and thorough.

"That way, please. You will lead; I will follow, of course."

"Of course," the Killmaster replied drily, and moved up the drive with the little man ten paces behind him. Just short of the front stoop, lights came on and the massive front door swung wide.

A tall, bull-necked man looking very uncomfortable in a tight-fitting suit scowled down at Carter.

"He was armed?" His words were directed at the guard, who had moved to the side.

"Yes, a gun and knife. I have them both."

"You checked for explosives?"

"*Oui, mon général*. The shoes and the belt are both genuine."

The big man swung his scowl back to Carter. "I am Omegla."

"I know, General," Carter said, dropping his hands to his sides. "Can we get on with this?"

"I want you to know that this meeting was arranged against my wishes."

Carter shrugged. "That's of no concern to me. I came to see President Goulanda. Do I see him or not?"

The glint in the other man's eyes was more curiosity than malice. He studied the AXE man for a few more seconds and then shrugged himself in resignation.

"Very well, this way."

They moved down a long hall, through a small anteroom,

and entered a beam-ceilinged study. Near a pair of tall, arched windows sat the president-in-exile of Togo.

As Carter approached him, the president stood. His hair was graying and his dark face was creased with deep lines that spoke as much of worry as age. Everything about him except his eyes looked tired.

The eyes looked wary and almost haunted.

"Monsieur le Président, I assure you, this is a pleasure."

Carter accepted the outstretched hand and noted with relief that the grip was firm and steady.

"You are not French."

"No," Carter replied and offered no more in the way of explanation.

The inference was not lost on the old man, and it brought a wan smile to his face. "I suppose, at this point, it does not really matter who or what you are . . . even Russian."

"I assure you, monsieur, I am not Russian."

Goulanda sat and motioned Carter to the opposite chair. Omegla remained standing, watchful, a few paces away.

"Your man's enticement was arms and funds for the reestablishment of my government."

"That is partially correct," Carter replied, sliding two neatly typed pages across the table. "I have prepared a shopping list for your and the general's approval."

Goulanda glanced over the pages and motioned Omegla forward. The general perused it with much more scrutiny and then lifted his puzzled eyes to bore in on Carter.

"I must say, this is very impressive but hardly possible given our current situation. I am sure, if you have gone this far, that you know that we escaped from the country with hardly any funds at all."

Carter ignored his words. "Do you have or can you amass the number of men to handle those arms?"

"We can," Omegla replied, "but that is not the problem."

"The problem, my mysterious friend," Goulanda offered,

"is credit. We don't seem to have the friends who are willing to finance us enough to purchase such vast quantities."

"Ah, but you do, monsieur."

Carefully Carter outlined Cyclops's role in the coup that had overthrown Goulanda's government. He explained the role the Russians had hoped to play and how the huge international company had managed to stop Moscow cold. Then he topped it all with the thick sheaf of papers he had gotten from Anthony Zorez.

As Goulanda read, life seemed to seep back into the old face. "My God, monsieur, are these authentic?"

"Absolutely. If they can be used properly for propaganda purposes just before you launch your attack, Tebessa will be completely undermined. You will have an internal revolution going before you even cross the frontier."

"Amazing," Goulanda replied, his shoulders rising to take shape again.

"Funding for the arms will be done through a completely private international firm. All that is needed from you is a paper stating that thirty million dollars of Cyclops money will be converted to a certain Swiss account once you seize the banks in your country."

A smile of understanding creased the old man's face. "I see. We use their money to finance their overthrow."

"Exactly."

"Monsieur," Omegla said, "the list of arms you have given us would amount to no more than fifteen million, top price."

"True," Carter replied, smiling himself now. "The investor, I think, is entitled to a generous profit. Don't you agree?"

The two men exchanged glances and Goulanda spoke. "Would you excuse us for a moment?"

"Certainly."

They moved across the room and spoke in hushed tones for several minutes. Carter leaned back in the chair with as bored an expression as he could muster on his face and lit a cigarette.

Of course he was taking a very long, long shot, but in the dark, that was the name of the game. He had to convince Chandra Braxton, a woman he did not know, had never met, and hardly traveled in the same circles with, to finance a revolution in a country that she had probably never heard of.

But if the profile fit, Madame Braxton would jump at the chance to create such a profit in return for manipulating a little hardware and risking a few million.

Goulanda was back, easing himself into his chair. This time Omegla also sat, to Carter's right.

"Needless to say, your proposition intrigues us."

"Monsieur le Président, if it did no more than intrigue you, you would not be sitting where you are right now. You have nothing to lose and a country to regain by going along with my offer. My only real stipulation is good faith in the repayment of the money once Togo is yours."

"And you are adamant about not revealing your affiliation or the source of the funds?"

"That is the only way it can be done. The ball, so to speak, is in your court."

Omegla couldn't resist jumping in. His eyes were on fire as he leaned over the table toward Carter. "How soon can we get the arms?"

"I would say a minimum of two weeks. I will contact you using the same method as before once I can tell you the actual date and be sure of it."

"You know, of course," Goulanda said, "that our neighbors have given us refuge only on consideration that we not use their countries as staging bases for a counterrevolution."

"I figured as much," Carter replied, "and I have taken that into account. Did you bring the maps?"

Omegla crossed the room and returned with a detailed topographical map of the western coast of Africa. He spread it out and bent a gooseneck lamp down over it.

Carter plotted longitude and latitude, then marked a position off the south coast of Ghana.

"Once the date is set, a freighter named the *Wayfarer Belle* will be anchored outside territorial waters—here."

"With the arms?"

"Yes, including the two helicopter gunships. Between now and then you and your people must gather enough small craft to ferry your whole army out to this position."

Omegla frowned and rubbed his chin with his right hand. "I am afraid I still don't understand."

"Arrangements will be made for the *Wayfarer Belle* to dock in Lomé just prior to dawn the day after taking your people aboard."

"We strike from the docks?"

"Yes," Carter said. "Total surprise coupled with the sympathy of the people should be enough. Also, with this amount of firepower, you will be nearly twice as strong as Tebessa's current forces."

Goulanda laid his hand on his general's shoulder. "Will it work, old friend?"

"It will work if the timing is right. Infantry, with the help of the gunships, can secure the dock area long enough to unload the tanks and the other heavy equipment."

"Also," Carter added, "if you set up your subversives somewhere in the north, here, I will arrange for an arms drop where you specify. As Tebessa retreats, you will have him in a vise."

"It will work," Omegla growled.

Carter took a typed agreement from his coat pocket and laid it on the table. "If you will sign this, Monsieur le Président, and you, General, witness it, I will be on my way."

Goulanda perused it and frowned. "There are no companies named—nothing but blanks in all the spaces for names except for ours."

"No, there are not. Do you care where the money goes if you have your country back?"

Again the two men exchanged a quick look.

Then they both signed.

THIRTEEN

Carter didn't even try to spot the person or persons who picked him up in the Athens air terminal. He was pretty sure someone at the Geneva airport had made the tag, checked his flight destination, and called ahead.

He didn't have time to play games with them, and besides, that was why he had summoned Leila to join him in Greece.

If she was half as good in Greece as she had been in Morocco, his back would be well covered.

He cabbed to the Hilton and checked in with his own passport. Tipping the bellboy in advance, he detoured to a bank of phone booths and consulted Mock's list. By this time he couldn't underestimate the cunning of Cyclops's forces. He was battling an equal and he knew it.

Better a public phone than the phone in his room.

"Yes?"

"Olympus, this is Drumbeat. Has she arrived?"

"Room Seven-twenty, the Hilton, under her own passport. As near as we have been able to ascertain, she was not followed and, as yet, has not been spotted."

"You pulled your people off as I requested?"

"Yes, but the general does not agree with you."

"Tell the general to have faith in his own people. That's why I've sent for Leila."

He killed the connection, thinking how odd this whole situation was. Working with the Russians was one thing. Working with them and having them concerned for your life was another.

He made a beeline for the elevator and his room. Once there he called the desk, got room service, and ordered a huge meal.

By the time he had changed clothes it had arrived. He tipped the waiter generously and gave him enough time to disappear before leaving the room.

All things considered, someone who had just ordered a huge hot meal would not be roaming around the hotel, let along hitting the town.

Carter's room was 914. He took the elevator down to the fifth floor and the service stairs back up to the seventh. The door to 720 was cracked an inch. He slipped inside and locked it behind him.

She was waiting in the alcove, a drink in each hand, a loosely belted robe around her glorious body, and a come-hither smile on her face.

She offered her lips, but Carter pecked her cheek and lifted one of the glasses from her hand.

"Business?" she said with a sigh.

"For now. Olympus says you got out of Casablanca clean. What do you say?"

"I'm sure of it," she replied, all business herself now. "And I'm sure I got into Greece just as clean. I took four flights and changed wigs twice. I used a private boat to come over from Italy."

"Good. I want you to dial this number and use this code. When it's answered, just hand the phone over to me."

She didn't question it. If there was a switchboard operator down below monitoring the calls from his room, this was the best dodge. And a man's voice had not originated this call.

"Here, Nick."

Carter grabbed the phone. Frank Layton was already on the other end of the line.

"Hello, hello . . ."

"Yes, Ambassador Layton, I'm here."

"Look, I don't know what the hell this is all about but—"

"But you have been informed of my request."

"Yes, and I've put it back through channels just to make sure someone at home hadn't gone nuts."

Carter smiled to himself. "And you were told . . . ?"

"To give you all the help I can."

"Then you—"

"But," came the interruption, "I want to warn you, our relations with Greece are shaky enough without you boys coming in and screwing things up . . ."

"There won't be any screwing up in Greece, I assure you, sir. Do you have a way of getting me to Chandra Braxton?"

There was a long pause on the other end of the line and then a sigh. "She's having a gathering on her yacht tomorrow evening. It's to be an all-night cruise out of Mykonos through the islands—mostly for business purposes and politics. One of my people is representing the embassy. You'll be her escort."

"And you have already informed the lady that I am legit and have clout?"

"I have relayed to the lady that you are one of our chief boogeymen. I hope that is sufficient for your nefarious purposes."

"That will be fine, sir," Carter replied, biting his lip to keep back the anger. "Thank you so very much for all your time and trouble."

The line went dead. Carter dropped the receiver.

"Bastard."

"The general has the same problems with Moscow. Sometimes I wonder why he puts up with it."

Carter mused on that one. "I've been wondering. Just what is your connection with them . . . idealism or money?"

"I grew up in the desert hating camels, filth, and not having enough to eat. Is that answer enough?"

"No."

"A pity. It's the only one I can offer. You are American. It is hard for you to understand."

Carter shrugged. "Enough said—let's get back to business. I want you to climb into something that will blend into the background . . . jeans or something peasanty."

"We're going hunting?"

"You are. I let Cyclops know that I know. My guess is that they are going to send someone after me. I want you to tag that someone."

"How?"

"They tail the bait . . . me. You spot them while I tour Athens and disappear."

"You're mad."

"Quite. Get dressed."

She shrugged out of the robe and, naked, walked to the closet.

"Jeans and peasant blouse coming up."

Carter played tourist, on foot, for a little over an hour. Then he hailed a cab and headed toward the south coast and Sounion. Once there he directed the driver to the foot of the Temple of Poseidon and the restaurant, Dimitri's.

Somewhere behind him he instinctively knew that there was someone out to kill him. Hopefully, somewhere behind that someone was Leila.

He always dined at Dimitri's at least once whenever he was in Athens. The owner, Dimitri Adopolous, was an old friend. And tonight Carter planned to call on that friendship to get him out of Athens unobserved and onto the island of Mykonos.

It was a wonderful old Greek mansion, modernized now, facing south and west toward the sea. It nestled in a grove of two-hundred-year-old olive trees that framed beautifully the long white building against the whiter beach and the deep aquamarine of the sea beyond.

Carter paid off the driver, making the tip well worth the

man's drive back to Athens. Before entering he cased the road both ways and the tightly packed buildings across the way. That, he thought, would be the ideal place. It was already crowded with fishermen, their wives, and a score of tourists.

Inside he was given a seaside table. Dimitri arrived with the menu.

"Old friend, it has been too long."

"Dimitri," Carter said, embracing the rotund man and returning the sloppy kisses on both cheeks. "Is your brood larger since last you fed me?"

"By two. Alas, more girls. I am bewitched it would seem. What will you eat?"

"Whatever you send. And Dimitri . . . ?"

"Yes?"

"A moment of your time for a bit of conversation over the meal?"

"Of course."

Nothing else needed to be said.

The dinner was superb but as usual more than any ten men could eat. Between the phyllo pastry layered with feta cheese and the lamb roasted with fresh herbs, Carter explained his needs.

"Do you still have the plane?"

"Of course," Dimitri said. "The fish and vegetables are still much cheaper and fresher if they are brought here daily from the outer islands."

Carter smiled but didn't state what was on his mind. Dimitri was far more than just a purveyor of fine cuisine. His American-built twin-engine Beechcraft did indeed make regular trips to the outer islands for fresh fish and produce. The plane also flew unannounced flights to Italy and North Africa for contraband a lot more valuable than foodstuffs.

"Would you be making a trip tonight, my friend?"

"I had nothing planned, but of course plans can always be made."

"I would like to make a little trip, very quietly."

"For you, Nicholas, a trip can always be arranged."

"I need to get to Mykonos without announcing it or going through any ports or terminals. I also need a quiet bed this evening and a place to spend the day tomorrow. Out of sight would be appreciated."

"Say no more. What time would you like to depart?"

Carter checked his watch. "Three hours at the most—about midnight?"

"Ayelos, my pilot, and the plane will be ready. You remember the strip—how to get there?"

"I do."

"After you arrive, Ayelos will take you to the house of my cousin on Mykonos."

"Dimitri, I believe you have a cousin on every one of the islands."

"Of course I do," the old thief replied with a wide smile. "Would that they were all members of the police. Then they would truly be treasured relations."

"And you would own Greece," Carter said with a laugh.

The Killmaster left the restaurant without attempting to pay for the meal. The old man would never have accepted a cent for his hospitality anyway.

He strolled to the nearby village and meandered for the better part of an hour. When he was pretty sure Leila had been given enough time to nail down his trackers, he entered a taverna on one of the smaller and darker side streets.

It was a fishermen's bar with a few tourists sprinkled among the natives. Carter took a seat in the darkest part of the room and ordered a beer.

Twenty minutes later Leila entered. She had acquired a bulky dark sweater that she now wore over her blouse. The curls of her blond wig barely showed under a knitted fisherman's cap.

Carter guessed that Leila had probably changed some part of her appearance at least twice already in the course of the evening.

She lingered by the windows for a couple of minutes and then headed for the rear of the room and the toilets.

Obviously, Carter thought, none of those present in the taverna were part of the pursuit team.

He waited until she had disappeared down a dark hall and then followed. Bypassing the men's room, he had to squint in the near darkness to recognize the designation on the door for the women's.

"All right?" he whispered.

"Yes."

He darted inside and closed the door behind him. "Did you get them spotted?"

"Yes. There are two—a man and a woman. They are very good, but both of them seem so intent on you that they made some mistakes. I was able to spot them the first hour in Athens after they picked you up."

Carter smiled. "I imagine they are intent because their boss has told them to take me out as soon as possible. Are you rigged?"

"Yes."

She pulled up the right sleeve of the sweater. Strapped to her right arm was a shiny steel tube about a foot long.

Carter knew the piece. It was a Welrod, probably the most effective assassination pistol in the world. It was developed in the naval gun factory in Washington during World War II. The French resistance had killed a lot of Nazi bigwigs with others just like the one Leila had strapped to her arm right now.

"Mean little piece," Carter said.

"And quiet."

"I know. Where are they now?"

"The man is at the open end of the street. He's wearing a leather vest over a dark blue shirt and light tan trousers."

"A car?"

"Yes, but he parked it right after you arrived and he hasn't gone back to it."

"And the woman?"

"She came down from Athens on a Vespa. Right now she has discarded her riding helmet and put a scarf, red, over her head. She is wearing dark gray slacks and a denim jacket. You'll spot her across the street haggling with a fruit vendor. The Vespa is parked right beside them."

"All right, here's how we go . . ."

In quick, terse sentences Carter outlined his plan. He had already spotted a dead-end alley in his previous walk. It was long with two sharp bends. It was also very narrow, fairly deserted, and other than one light at its end, dark.

Leila indicated that she could find it without trouble and checked the hall.

"It's clear."

"I'll give you twenty minutes to get in place."

"Right."

Carter returned to the barroom. Leila would exit by the taverna's rear door and make her way to the designated place.

The Killmaster gave her the allotted twenty minutes and then left himself to become the bait.

The woman was gone, but Carter spotted the man in the tan pants within fifty paces. He was industriously talking to a young hooker, and from the look on the girl's bored face, he wasn't coming up with nearly enough money.

Carter made a long, swinging arc toward the beach and then came back toward the center of the village. Twice, on slightly more quiet streets, he thought he heard the gentle purr of a Vespa behind him but didn't pause to check.

The important thing was that they were following him, probably in alternating shifts. It wasn't important, at this point, that he spot them.

When he hit the narrow, alleylike street he speeded up. Behind him he could hear the dull thud of his tracker's footsteps. He and the woman had followed him earlier, so they also knew about the dead-end aspect of the alley.

They were going to take him . . . or try. That was fairly

obvious from the elephantine tread that was now sounding behind him.

Carter slowed around the first curve for a few paces and then began to sprint. The thudding footsteps speeded up to match his pace.

"Come on, boy, come on," Carter whispered to himself.

Just past the second curve he slowed again. The pace of his pursuing friend didn't slacken. The Killmaster tuned his ears to detect the woman's lighter tread, but it wasn't there.

Surely in a boxed-in alley they would both come for him at the same time.

No matter, he thought. The plan couldn't be changed now.

The alley ended in a house-lined courtyard and a high brick wall. The whole was illuminated by one very dim streetlight that threw a perfect circle at its base.

Carter got to the center of the courtyard, still short of the pool of light, and activated the spring that shot Hugo into his right hand. He whirled, dropped into a crouch, and waited.

Tan Pants bolted around the curve, saw Carter, and came ahead into the clearing without a moment's hesitation. When he reached the outer limits of the illumination, the Killmaster saw why. He was armed with an ugly curved Curae knife in each hand. And from the way he moved in, Carter knew that this boy knew how to use both of them.

Carter avoided a double thrust and managed a quick jab on his own to put the other man on guard.

Around and around they went like two feinting boxers, but the man didn't come in again.

And then Carter realized why. He was being systematically moved backward and to his right, directly into the pool of light beneath the streetlamp.

He tried to change direction, but the slashing knives did their work. Twice the deadly blades got to his flapping jacket, no skin but a lot of shredded material.

And then, just as the two of them hit the circle of light, the night exploded.

It was the sharp chatter of a machine pistol, its slugs raising hell with the wall behind Carter. It was a stitching burst designed to waste anything and anyone that lay in its path.

It got Tan Pants first.

His body practically exploded and came through the air toward Carter.

The Killmaster embraced the corpse and fell using the dead man as a shield. Around the body he saw her.

She was on the roof, a slight figure outlined against the night sky. She was firing from the hip like a pro, the gun belching orange flame in a nonstop pattern.

At the same time Carter saw Leila emerge from a nearby doorway. She ran in a crouch toward the opposite side of the courtyard where she could get a clearer shot with the Welrod.

The running figure caught the woman's eye long enough to perplex her into a firing pause.

Carter took the few seconds' pause to pull Wilhelmina from under his left armpit. He rested the barrel on the dead man's shoulder and fired at the streetlamp.

It took four tries, and then he only scored a hit when the fourth slug careened around the inside of the downward reflector and finally burst the bulb.

Instantly he rid himself of the body, rolled to his feet, and sprinted for the wall directly beneath the woman.

It was clear now: Tan Pants, though he probably hadn't known it himself, was a decoy. The poor bastard had been told to set Carter up for a clear shot by getting him into the light and then get out of the way himself.

Only the female shooter on the roof had never planned to give him time to get out of the way.

To get Carter, Tan Pants was expendable.

The woman above him now was a very nasty lady.

But Carter and Leila had an advantage. They were in a well of darkness. Every time she raised up to fire she would be outlined against the sky.

A good five minutes had elapsed since her first burst.

Greek police in small villages are pretty tolerant, but not that much.

It was only a matter of time before they would have visitors.

Carter popped out, fired, and melted back against the building. The answering burst from the machine pistol was immediate.

He could see Leila in her doorway and the shooter couldn't. She was lining up the Welrod. Leila had gotten the message.

Again he popped out, fired, and drew fire from the chatter gun. Twice more he performed the operation.

And then he heard the familiar sound of the Welrod. It was like the soft popping of a champagne cork.

There was a growling whine from above and then the machine pistol clattered at Carter's feet.

"You got her!"

"I think I only winged her," Leila replied.

The sound of running feet over gravel on the roof above them told the tale. If Leila had winged her, it hadn't been a good enough shot to stop her from running.

"Come on!" Carter growled.

Together they charged back toward the open end of the alley.

Carter had already put it all together. The woman, when she figured Carter's direction, had sent Tan Pants on in. Then she had climbed to the roofs from another street.

"Go on around," Carter hissed. "I'll go up and over."

Leila bolted toward a corner and Carter cut back toward the buildings. As he ran he discarded Wilhelmina's nearly empty magazine and jacked in a fresh one.

He headed for a fire escape that crept like a thin spider web up the side of the end building. Just as he reached the bottom rung he heard the dull sound of an engine come to life.

"Nick, she's coming back your way!"

The cry was barely out of Leila's mouth when around the

corner of the building came the Vespa with the small figure leaning far forward over the machine's handlebars.

His decision as to what to do was made for him.

A slug hit sharply two feet above his head, the brickwork showering into fragments.

Carter dived, bringing Wilhelmina up at the same time. But the speeding Vespa was going by too fast and weaving at the same time.

He got off three worthless shots and then stood cursing as the little machine skidded around a corner and was gone.

"Nick?"

"Yeah," he grunted, jogging toward the end of the building and the sound of Leila's voice.

She was just around the corner, playing a small penlight across the pavement.

"Look here."

Carter followed the trail she made with the light. There were spots of fresh blood every few inches leading from a fire escape to a thick hedge.

"She had the Vespa waiting," Carter said.

"I did get her," Leila commented. "She's not down, but she's hurt."

"And she won't be tracking me anymore tonight. I've got a private plane ride to Mykonos. You get back to Athens. Get your things and head for Casablanca. I'll know by this time tomorrow night if we've got our supplier."

"You'll call me at the villa?"

"Right. From there let's hope it's a go and you can contact your rebels."

"Nick, she's wounded. If I look hard enough, I might be able to find her yet tonight in Athens."

"Don't bother. I've got a hunch she's going to find us again."

FOURTEEN

The *Noble Savage* was big, posh, and built for speed and total comfort.

Carter nursed a scotch on the stern and waited, like the others, for the appearance of the great lady herself.

Above the gliding boat the night was clear and beautiful with sparkling stars. Beneath his feet the steady throb of a pair of perfectly tuned Deutz marine diesels pushed the boat's gleaming prow out of Mykonos's harbor toward the open sea at a steady eighteen knots.

Around him, tuxedoed men and elegantly gowned and coiffed women sipped Dom Perignon as if it were water and discussed their favorite subject, money.

All of them, young or old, were serene and confident, full of that assurance that great wealth and position confers.

"Mr. Carter . . . ?"

"Yes, Effie?"

"What should I do?"

"Mingle, Effie, just mingle and do whatever it is the ambassador wanted you to do."

"Yes, yes, I'll do that. Will you be all right? Oh, dear, that was a dreadfully stupid question, wasn't it?"

"Not at all, Effie. I'll be fine, you just go ahead."

Effie McCann was a small, rather plain woman with wide,

searching eyes and an awe of the glittering world her brilliant brain had brought her into.

When Carter had met her earlier that evening at the prearranged place, she had been shaking like a leaf.

"I've never been on a date with a spy before. How do you do, Mr. Carter?"

"It's Nick and I do fine, Miss McCann, and so will you. Just be yourself. And by the way, spies aren't all they're cracked up to be."

Now, as her slim figure moved away through the crowd, Carter thought how much more real and reliable Effie McCann probably was than the pompous men and overdone woman she had to smile at and make small talk with this night.

Suddenly a hush fell over the crowd. Carter turned forward toward the superstructure and saw why.

Their hostess was making her appearance on the upper deck. One look and the Killmaster could see why Chandra Braxton held such sway over so many people.

She was dressed in a gown of white satin, its one shoulder clasp a solid gold reproduction of a piece of ancient Greek jewelry. The cascading fabric showed off a body whose beauty had not diminished with age. Her appearance was as impressive as her reputation. Basically it was a simple dress, but Chandra Braxton somehow made it seem absolutely regal and as timeless as the Aegean.

Her hair was short and dark with twin streaks of gray at the sides, flowing back over small, pert ears. Deep green eyes stared from an almost but not quite classical face. The mouth was a little too full and the nose was a little too large.

Chandra Braxton's beauty, Carter decided, was harsh. But, then, so was its owner.

She moved with the grace of a queen down the ladder and began to greet her guests.

Carter moved forward, following her at a distance, listening, weighing the choice Yvonne had made.

Within an hour he knew that this woman was perfect for

the operation. In that time she charmed leading industrialists from four countries, all in their own languages, renewed several contracts with political figures from two other nations, and probably enriched her corporation by at least ten million dollars.

A pretty good hourly wage, Carter thought. It would have to be more than just money to get this powerful woman excited about any project.

By the time she had made her way around to the lesser mortals such as Effie McCann, Carter had moved beside his "date."

"And this is Nicholas Carter, Mrs. Braxton," Effie said, only a slight tremble in her voice. "He's new . . . with the Agency."

"Yes, Ambassador Layton has acquainted me with Mr. Carter's qualifications. I am so happy you could join us this evening, Mr. Carter."

"Thank you, Mrs. Braxton. You have a lovely boat."

"We like to call them yachts."

"Sorry."

"Are you enjoying our little soiree?" she asked, lowering her voice seductively.

"Not in the least," Carter replied without the least change of expression.

"Oh?"

"Talk of money bores me."

Her laugh was low, throaty, and genuine. "I'm glad we have a minority representative aboard. Perhaps later we can discuss matters other than money."

"I would enjoy that."

Chandra Braxton glided away and Carter turned to Effie, who looked as if she had just been struck by an ax.

"Something wrong?"

"I've never heard anyone talk to Chandra Braxton like that before."

He chuckled. "I'll bet she hasn't either."

Carter freshened his drink from the tray of a passing

steward and moved to the bow.

He felt downright elated. Chadron wasn't as big and powerful as Cyclops, but he reasoned that if he could acquire
Chandra Braxton's help, the game would still be even.
Somehow he knew that this woman was capable of matching
wits and style with anyone, even the powers behind Cyclops.

Almost an hour passed before he sensed her approach and
turned to meet her.

"You make a very striking figure against the sea, Mr.
Carter. In fact you fit my idea of a spy perfectly."

"Thank you. I always hate to fall short of the image I am
supposed to have."

"Frank Layton hates your guts. He says you are an amoral,
dangerous man."

"The ambassador has a right to his own opinion. I admire
the way you handle the moguls."

She blinked at his sudden change of direction, but only
once, and came right back.

"Business and more business. I am afraid it is a rather
boring twenty-four-hour occupation after you have reached
the level I have reached."

"One that you revel in, I'm sure."

She had been gazing out to sea. Now she turned her green,
penetrating eyes on him and let her full lips part in a blazing
smile.

"But one that does become boring. That is why I agreed to
see you when Frank asked. Particularly after he warned me
not to."

She moved to his side until her shoulder touched his and
she gripped the rail with both hands.

Carter did the same and together they watched the edge of
the *Noble Savage*'s prow knife through the Aegean, sending
two perfect curls rippling aft to become foaming wake.

"What do you want, Mr. Carter?"

"Your brain, your power, your expertise, and the use of
some of your money."

She laughed. "Well, that is about everything except my body."

"I don't think I could handle that, too, along with all the rest," he said with a chuckle.

Out of the corner of his eye he could see the smile melt from her lips, and her knuckles, gripping the rail, grew white.

"What do you say we stop fencing."

"Fencing?"

"Man-woman fencing. Little word games. It doesn't take a genius to figure that a man like you doesn't waste his time playing in the sandbox when there is a great big beach out there. What the hell do you want with me?"

"I want to start a war, a counterrevolution really."

"Where?"

"I can't tell you that unless you agree to help."

"Not exactly fair but nevertheless intriguing. Just where do I come in?"

Carter turned to face her. She moved at the same time, and for the first time he suddenly realized how tall she was. Their eyes were nearly on a level.

He withdrew a copy of the arms list he had shown to Omegla and Goulanda in Geneva and pressed it into her hand. In seconds she had taken it in and, he was pretty sure, calculated her ability to fill it and the cost.

"Jesus Christ."

"It will be a fairly good-sized revolution," he said drily. "Can you fill that list?"

"I assume you wouldn't want new goods."

"Absolutely not. It's my understanding that new goods can't be hidden."

"No, not very easily. It will take a little time on the computer, but overall, yes, I think it can be done."

"There are a few stipulations beyond the buy," he said, lighting two cigarettes and handing her one of them. "The arms, the method of purchase, and the money that buys them must be completely untraceable, literally laundered before delivery.''

"Go on.''

"There must be no end-use certificates beyond a certain point.''

"That wouldn't be a new twist in this business,'' she replied. "I am still listening.''

"It's worth thirty million. Whatever you pay for the arms is up to you.''

Now the green eyes narrowed and the tongue came out to dart over her full lips. "You are either a damned fool or someone has one hell of a lot of money they don't give a damn about.''

"Neither. Let's just say that if our little coup is successful, there will be much more than that amount available to the winner.''

She paused, her eyes slits now, studying him. He could almost sense the digits and tumblers of her computerlike mind spinning before she spoke again.

"That sounds like a hitch—'if our little coup is successful.' Is that a way of saying it might not be?''

"Nothing is sure. A hitch? Only a little one: you have to supply the original buy money, and you don't get it and the profit back until after the war. But there is some insurance. I have a signed I.O.U.''

"You are insane.''

"A little. It helps in this business. But I think you've already decided to take the deal. You're a gambler.''

She hedged. "Maybe so, but your connection with Frank Layton tells me you are with an important agency. He almost said so. The U.S. government must be backing this.''

"No way, Mrs. Braxton. I have to stress that. You take the deal and it blows, Uncle Sam has never heard of either one of us, or of the toys.''

"Good God, that is an enormous risk when we are talking about these figures.''

"It sure as hell is." He grasped her hand and lightly brushed his lips across the back of it. "But then just living is one hell of a risk."

"You are a con man as well, but a charming one. Very well, I like the gamble."

"Welcome aboard."

"We cannot do much tonight. I have guests. Besides, you look exhausted."

"I am."

"My chief steward will make you comfortable in one of the cabins. Tomorrow morning, when everyone is off the ship, we will do a search and see if we can find the goods. Deal?"

"Deal."

He watched her move away and wondered what she would have said if he had suggested she throw in her body along with everything else.

"It's me, Marcus."

"Where are you?"

"In Rome. I missed him, or I should say them."

"Damn, damn, damn!"

"And I was wounded."

"How bad?" There was no alarm or concern in the voice, only a note of petulance.

"My right forearm. It isn't bad, but I lost a lot of blood. I left Greece at once without even going back to Athens. It was just too dangerous."

"How did it happen?"

"Carter had help with him I didn't know about—a woman."

"It was probably the Arab bitch Serge spotted in Casablanca. Our people there lost her. Our move to Togo is complete now, so there is not a great deal one man or even several can do."

"I'm sorry, Marcus. I have failed."

"It is all right, my dear. It is partially my fault anyway. I am afraid I have underestimated this Carter."

"What do you wish me to do?"

"Come home. We will just have to wait for the next time he turns up. When you arrive we will plan a full-scale attack in preparation for that time."

"I will leave at once. Good-bye, Marcus."

"Good-bye, my dear."

Marga Lund hung up the phone and stared at it.

If there was a next time, she wondered.

For the first time in her life, Marga felt fear.

Could this man Carter be the one, the one all the old pros told her she would one day meet?

Could this Carter be the man who would be able to kill her before she could kill him?

FIFTEEN

Carter was picking over a much-too-large breakfast when Chandra Braxton appeared on deck the next morning.

She was dressed casually in a pair of revealing shorts and a skimpy halter. He stared at her unabashedly and smiled. The two-piece costume barely contained enough material to make a child's playsuit.

"Morning."

"Good morning."

She stood directly in front of him with no self-consciousness in her near nudity and calmly returned his gaze.

"What are you thinking?"

"That you're a marvelously preserved woman."

She threw back her head and roared with laughter. "No wonder I liked you the first moment I saw you. You may be dangerous, a scoundrel as Layton has said, but you are honest. I went to work on the machines as soon as my guests departed at dawn. I think I've located the goods."

It was the Killmaster's turn to blink. And then he realized. She had been up all night and was still ready to go. Also, she must have a total computer system operative on the *Noble Savage*.

"You've got computers on board?"

"It is the modern age," she replied, folding into the deck

161

chair beside him. "I have computers like your president has his little red phone . . . everywhere."

"How much were you able to locate?"

"Everything."

Carter swallowed hard but managed to contain his amazement. "You mean the whole list?"

"Down to the last mortar and nine-millimeter bullet."

"Even the tanks?"

"Even the two helicopters," she replied with a chuckle, obviously enjoying the impact her news had on this usually unflappable man. "I have two sellers, one in Egypt and one in Somalia, who can fill the whole bill."

"They're updating their equipment," Carter said flatly.

"Of course. The small arms are M-twenty-one automatic rifles."

"Swedish?"

"Yes. I also have a line on Carl Gustaf nine-millimeter submachine guns that are being upgraded. Those are from the Egypt originator."

"And Egypt is buying the replacements from . . . ?" Carter asked.

"Chadron," she said with a wide smile. "Are there any objections?"

"To you and your corporation making another easy half million on the replacement sale? No, none at all. In fact, m'lady, me hat is off t'ya."

"Good. Now let's get the heart of the mystery solved. Just who am I working for?"

Carter passed the agreement he had obtained from Goulanda across the table. He waited until she had read it completely and digested it before he spoke.

"All you have to do is fill in the blanks. Any objections to the style or wording?"

"None. One of my holding companies in Switzerland or the Netherlands Antilles will be the original purchaser. Then I'll launder them through Belgium. After the ownership is established and then transferred again, they'll disappear."

"You sound like you know what you're doing."

"I didn't get this yacht for Christmas, Carter. I got it with my brains."

Carter knew she was oh so right.

The merchandising of arms worldwide is a multimillion-dollar business. It is not for the weak of heart or the slow of brain or foot. The buying or selling of weaponry, from a handgun to a rocket launcher to a used tank, takes cunning, deviousness, guts, and one hell of a lot of cash.

Obviously Chandra Braxton had it all, in spades.

"All I will need from you is a phony company to toss the cash around in and act as paymaster at the end."

"Say no more." He dropped the packet of documents containing the Liechtenstein incorporation and Swiss bank account on Togland Ltd. in front of her. "I took the trouble to have that set up a few days ago. There is one million in seed money in there that I would like back when the time comes."

She scanned it briefly and shook her head. "You counted on me all the time."

"Let's say I was ninety percent sure."

"All right, Carter, let's go down to the computer room and go to work."

It was a high-tech wonderland or nightmare, depending on one's expertise in the field. The ship's main salon had been redesigned into a computer layout that made most bank systems seem small and/or cumbersome. Everything, as near as the Killmaster could tell from his knowledge, was state-of-the-art.

In seconds, even at sea, Chandra Braxton would be on-line to anywhere in the world with either the computers or one of two telex machines.

She introduced Carter to her code man and her systems coordinator, and then they all sat down and went to work.

As they progressed, the woman explained in detail each step they took.

Throughout the world Chadron had branch offices or independent agents for the buying and selling of arms.

The chief job these agents had was to spot surplus arms before they came on the market. They would then feed their information into Chadron's home office so a buy or trade could be arranged before a smart competitor could make the deal.

"I'm going to use Hermelin Import-Export in Brussels as the final receiver. They have absolutely no conection to Chadron. In fact," she said with a chuckle, "Hermelin has no connection to anyone except a Luxembourg shell corporation and a Swiss safe-deposit box."

Carter read the telex messages going out and those coming in. Quickly he realized what the woman had already done.

"I guess you were pretty sure of me as well," he said.

"Oh? You mean you have figured it out?"

"You tendered an offer on all the arms earlier this morning, didn't you?"

She nodded. "I received a reply just before I came on deck to join you, some nonsense that the offer had been tendered and was being given every consideration."

"That's nonsense?"

"Oh, yes. Reading between the lines, it means someone wants a little extra or, in this case, *baksheesh*. I told my agent in Cairo to spread around two hundred thousand dollars American and not a penny more."

"Will that be enough? I mean, for a buy this size?"

"From me it will," she replied. "I have a reputation for paying up front in cash. In this business that is very important. When it comes to guns, no one trusts anyone else. That is because all of us are thieves at heart or a little shady at best. Credit is a fool's dream. Cash, quick cash, works wonders."

"It's coming through on the telex, Ms. Braxton," the assistant said.

"Read it to me as you decode it," she replied, calmly lighting a cigarette.

"Sale, all units confirmed . . . Must stipulate, repeat,

must stipulate . . . seller insists all units are to be invoiced through the United States . . . Will you agree? . . . If so, confirm for final confirmation this end."

She blew a perfect smoke ring and laughed. "Cowards. They want it that way because the Egyptian bigwigs selling the surplus arms do not want the responsibility of knowing when the arms are going to be sold or to whom they will be sold. If they are invoiced through the States, then they figure it is your problem to police where they end up."

"Should I send, Ms. Braxton?"

"Go ahead. Agree and also ask for full confirmation as soon as possible."

"What now?" Carter asked.

She moved into the console seat herself. "Now, we clean them up."

"Before you get confirmation?"

"I will get it."

For the next three hours Carter sat, watching her manipulate with awe and admiration.

First she made up a purchase order from Chadron of Canada to the Egyptian government for the agreed-upon price of the arms plus the bribe money and the Cairo agent's commission. It would all be submitted through the agent, who would deduct and forward the funds.

Next came a purchase order from Chadron, Inc. in New York to Chadron of Canada for the arms. In doing this she broke the purchase down by single units to save future tariff charges in the United States.

Carter did a little mental figuring and couldn't stop grinning. "You're amazing. By my calculations you just saved yourself three hundred thousand dollars on import duties by reporting them one piece at a time."

She shrugged. "A law is a law, especially when it works your way. Besides, the bribe money had to come from somewhere."

All the heavy equipment such as tanks, half-tracks, and

even the helicopters would be invoiced similarly but with a designation that they were being shipped directly to South America to be sold for scrap.

Ten minutes later the confirmation came through from Chadron of Canada. It took another five for Canada to sell the arms to Chadron, Inc. in New York.

"Read me those numbers on the Togland account in Switzerland."

Carter gave them to her, and her fingers began to fly over the keyboard.

"There," she said at last and stood. "Togland is now eleven and a half million richer by a loan from Hermelin. It will take about an hour for New York to get their money to Cairo. We can finish up then. Shall we go on deck and have some lunch?"

Over a lunch of lobster and a dry, slightly bitter local wine, they chatted about everything but the project.

Slowly, for some reason Carter couldn't understand, she turned the conversation to herself. She spoke of her childhood, her father, and her millions.

And the more she spoke, opening herself up to him for no reason he could understand, he found himself liking her.

"The file I read on you . . ." he interjected in a brief lull.

"Yes?"

"It said you rarely, in fact hardly ever leave Mykonos."

Her eyes fell and she grew pensive. "I suppose it is because I have already been everywhere and done most everything. I just don't have anyplace anymore that I have a desire to get back to."

"That's a pretty sad commentary for a woman with billions."

"Is it? I don't think so. Making money is all I know even though I have rather lost interest in the game."

"Then why do you keep doing it?"

Her head snapped up and for a brief instant there was fire, almost anger, in her eyes. Then they softened and she smiled.

"I could and will ask you the same question. Why, Mr.

Carter, do you keep doing what you do?''

"Touché."

"No, I mean it. I think I'm a pretty good judge of people. My guess is you're not just a spy. I think you're some kind of a special spy, or more. Do you kill people?''

He tensed slightly but didn't break, nor did the expression on his face alter.

"Sometimes," he replied truthfully.

"I thought so. And you've been doing it for a very long time, haven't you."

"Longer than I care to remember."

"Very well, then. The law of averages will one day catch up with you. Why don't you get out before it does and someone kills you?''

He sipped from his glass of wine for several moments, musing.

She waited patiently, watching his face until he was ready to give her an answer.

"Have you ever read Housman?''

"The English poet?''

"Yes.''

"Sorry. I'm afraid I leave little time for reading. I'm not an intellectual.''

"Neither am I, but someone once quoted me these lines and they've stuck in my head. It seems to be the best answer I can come up with for your question. You see, like you, I guess I'm too old and I've been at it too long to quit now.''

"Bullshit.''

"No. Let me tell you what Housman wrote. 'Life, to be sure, is nothing much to lose; but young men think it is, and once we were young . . .''

"And now you're too old . . . all the more reason—''

"Shhh, let me tell you the rest. I'll skip to the end. 'Their shoulders held the sky suspended; they stood, and earth's foundations stayed; what God abandoned, these defended and saved the sum of things for pay.' ''

"That sounds like . . .''

"It is," Carter replied, taking her hand and gently pulling her to her feet. "It's an epitaph for mercenaries. C'mon, Mrs. Braxton, let's go back to work."

When they returned to the computer room, the Chadron, Inc. funds had been transferred to the Cairo agent.

"Okay," she said, grim satisfaction in her voice. "Now comes the shift."

When the invoice had been cleared through New York, she put yet another purchase order into the works. This one from Hermelin in Brussels. This purchase order, in its entirety, was registered as "a buy for field scrap."

"Does that mean they have already disappeared?" Carter asked.

"Not quite. They will go from Hermelin to Togland. You are sure that there is absolutely no trace possible on Togland?"

"None," Carter said, and smiled. "That, I know just how to do."

"Good," she said, chuckling herself. "Then none of us or this can be traced."

"Just covering your ass, lady."

"Just covering my ass, lad."

"What's next?"

"What are your freighter's registration numbers, call frequencies, and name?"

"It's the *Wayfarer Belle*," Carter replied, and gave her the rest of the information.

In ten minutes the code man was back. "The *Wayfarer Belle* has accepted the coded order. She's on her way to the port of Alexandria."

Chandra Braxton sat back with a contented sigh. She had done her work well.

The entire transaction, from the initial bid through Cairo to the ownership of the arms by Hermelin of Brussels—a company with no Chadron connection—had taken place while the goods never moved from Alexandria, Egypt.

The last and final shift, which would thoroughly confound anyone trying to trace this transfer, was the last buy of the arms by Togland from Hermelin.

This was just completed when one of the telex machines started banging again.

The assistant decoded the message and handed it to Chandra Braxton. She scanned it quickly and handed it to Carter.

It was the confirmation of sale and full payment from Cairo.

"All right, Carter, you have your toys. Now go start our little war."

SIXTEEN

The following two days were a whirlwind of start-and-stop activity. It was rather like the army game: hurry up and wait.

During this time Carter was able to stay almost entirely out of sight through the aid of Chandra Braxton.

She had homes or apartments all over the world, and where she didn't she had discreet friends.

And with the use of her private jet and pilot he was able to move without hitting any large commercial airports.

The wind-down was a flight into the southern Sahara and a meet with Leila and an aging rebel named Habin el-Hassar.

It took the better part of a day talking and a great deal of baksheesh, but at last the man agreed to safely ferry the small arms across the desert.

From there Leila was dropped in Casablanca and given the code to contact Goulanda and General Omegla. Carter had already contacted Rowland and arranged for a meeting in a small out-of-the-way hotel near the foothills of the Atlas Mountains beyond Fez. This hotel would also be his and Leila's hiding place until jump-off time.

The morning after he arrived, Carter left his bungalow and entered the tiny dining room. He found the gambler outside. He was in the only available piece of shade on the terrace.

"Morning."

"Ahhh, aggg."

171

"You just get here?"

"Hour . . . ago."

Rowland sat, mummified, staring at a glass of juice by his left hand and a cup of thick coffee by his right. He looked like death on the half shell, and even his good eye was dulled.

"You're not talkative in the mornings, I take it," Carter said, sliding his chair into a tiny portion of Rowland's shade.

"Not when I'm dying," he replied, finally choosing the juice and bringing it up to his lips with both hands.

"*Café*," Carter told the buxom waitress, and Rowland groaned.

They sat in silence for several moments. Carter was waiting for the other man to start the conversation, but when he didn't, the Killmaster started musing aloud.

"Did you know that from that mountain, right over there, a mere handful of Berber tribesmen once held off the whole French foreign legion for over two years?"

"Oh."

"You're not a history buff, Rollo. I can tell," Carter said with a low laugh.

"No, I am not a goddamned history buff. I am a here-and-now buff. And right now I am dying . . . or flying. I can't exactly tell which."

"Flying? Well, you do look a little ill . . . in fact your color could pass for downright green."

Rowland moaned, sipped a little more of the life-giving fruit juice, moaned again, and painfully turned his head to face Carter.

"Not ill, my man. Wasted. Do you know that there are Arabs in this world who cannot do a half-hour's business without sucking up at least four or five pipes of hashish?—Do you know that? And do you know what? I met every one of those bastards last night."

"And . . ."

"You have no pity at all for my mental and physical condition, do you?"

"Can't say as I do, my friend. What happened?"

"We're set. The *Wayfarer Belle* docks day after tomorrow in Casablanca. The custom's inspector has been taken care of. The small stuff will be cleared and transferred to a warehouse. It will then be recrated as saddles and trucked. Ten miles outside the city the trucks will be hijacked."

"You have the men and the trucks?"

"More than enough."

"And you know where to meet the rebels?"

Rowland nodded with a pained look on his face.

"Good enough." Carter passed a slip of paper across the table. "There's the deposit slip for the rest of your money in your Swiss account with a bonus. As soon as the small stuff is back on the *Wayfarer Belle*, your job is over."

"Yeah, I know."

For the first time since Carter had joined him, Rowland completely raised his head. His watery eye scanned the few occupied tables and then turned to the Killmaster.

"You know something . . . I'd kind of like to join you and the chick in that airplane when the freighter's loaded."

"You're not serious."

"I am. I can make it back here to Fez in plenty of time before the *Belle* sails down the coast or you're ready to take off."

Carter eyed him closely. Chandra Braxton had already agreed to let Carter use her plane and pilot one more time for a Togo flyover just before the dawn invasion.

The plan was to drop Carter and Leila near Lomé so they could make their way to the offices of the state bank before all hell broke loose that morning.

Not only did Carter want to tie up the Cyclops funds before they could be transferred outside the country, he also wanted the company records. If he had those, he had the name of the head of the Cyclops monster. Once the coup was complete, Goulanda would take care of the underlings.

But Carter wanted the head man. Whoever he was, he was a rich and smart bird and completely ruthless when going after what he wanted. There was a good chance he could start over if he remained alive.

The Killmaster meant to make sure that didn't happen.

"Any special reason, Rollo?"

"Sure. I haven't had a good friggin' war in a long time.
And besides, I've never knocked over a bank. I think it's
about time I did. How about it?"

"You ever jump before?"

"Hell no, but I fell out of a tree once when I was a kid.
Same thing, isn't it?"

Carter laughed aloud. "Sure. It's even easier when you do
it with a chute."

"You've got a point there. Deal?"

"Deal. Welcome aboard."

The Killmaster walked him out to his car.

"Be back here by evening in three days. We take off for a
private strip in Liberia the next morning. Twenty-four hours
later we go in to Lomé from there."

"I'll be here."

Carter moved back through the parking lot. Just before
reaching the doors he noticed the car. It was the little white
Fiat Leila had used to leave the strip outside Casablanca. She
was here.

He moved through the hotel, crossed the courtyard, and
knocked before entering the bungalow.

She had already unloaded the bags and trunks, undressed,
and slipped into a cool robe.

"Rowland got the men?"

"He did," Carter replied with a laugh. "And a monumen-
tal hashish hangover. You made the connection?"

"Smooth as silk. Omegla is confirmed. They will be all
ready to go in more than enough time. Goulanda will fly in
just as soon as it's safe."

"Did General Mock come through for us?"

She knelt and opened two oversize suitcases at the foot of
the bed. In one was a pair of knocked-down AK-47 assault
rifles with enough ammunition to hold off all of Tebessa's

army. In the other were wraparound belts with grenades, a grenade launcher, and a mortar with shells.

Carter nodded with satisfaction. "If we can't take the bank with all that, we can't take anything."

Suddenly she stood, turning as she moved, and slid into his arms. The swift, soft placement of her warm mouth on his sent waves of pleasure through Carter's body. He moved his lips away and then quickly back again.

At the same time he felt the rest of her body moving against him and felt his own response.

Suddenly she broke the embrace, moved around him to the door, and locked it. She turned and leaned against it with her hips and breasts jutting toward him through the thin robe.

"How much time do we have?"

"Three days, give or take," he replied.

"And we shouldn't move out of the room for more than just meals. Right?"

"That's just about the size of it," Carter replied, feeling the heat flow through his body.

"Then," she said, shrugging the robe from her shoulders, "let's not waste the time."

The twin jets screamed as the powerful little plane lifted off and climbed into the night sky over the Atlantic. It was a cloudless night, but with any luck the hills between Lomé and the landing spot Omegla had given them would hide the signal flares.

Carter crouched between the two pilots.

"I'll move out to sea a bit to make it look good before I lose some altitude and head back in toward the coast and Lomé," the chief pilot said.

Carter nodded. "Good. You have a fix on the *Wayfarer Belle*?"

The young copilot checked his charts. "Right. She should be somewhere here, just off to starboard in a couple of minutes."

Carter wriggled himself and his gear to one of the starboard windows.

It wasn't long before he saw her. She was a big old rust bucket, but that made little difference.

The landing boats were already in the water and standing off. The freighter was making its turn in toward Lomé and Carter could see the troops massing on the decks.

He scooted back to the pilots. "They're going in. We can make our move anytime you're ready."

"Ready as ever."

He banked in a wide arc and immediately began losing altitude as he reached for the radio dials to change his frequency to Lomé.

Carter moved to a seat near the rear hatch. Leila and Rowland were already there. She was calmly smoking a cigarette; he was sweating blood.

"You okay?" Carter asked him.

"No, I'm not okay."

"Don't worry," Leila told him. "Once your chute opens, you just float like a feather."

"*If* the goddamned thing opens. And besides, going down isn't what bothers me. It's landing."

"Just bend your knees, relax, and roll when you hit," Carter said. "Don't land stiff."

"Relax, my man says. If I relax I'll wet my pants."

Carter adjusted his saddle straps and wriggled his shoulders to settle the chute more comfortably on his back as he sat. Then he took the phones from above the hatch and put them over his ears.

He had barely flicked on the switch when he heard the pilot's voice, speaking in French, trying to bring up the Lomé controller.

"Lomé . . . Lomé, this is I-N-T Four-niner-four-niner . . ."

"This is Lomé. Go ahead, Four-niner-four-niner."

"I'm on a night flight break-in for my second officer,

Lomé. We are experiencing some radar problems. Do you read?"

"I read. What's your problem?"

"Can't exactly tell without taking a ground look. Request permission for a set-down in your field, Lomé."

"One moment."

There was a click. "Are you on, Carter?"

"I'm here."

"What if he says no and sends me to Lagos?"

"Give him the international courtesy bit. Tell him you don't want to go back over the water again without proper radar."

"Right on."

Another click and Lomé came back on.

"Four-niner-four-niner?"

"I'm on, Lomé."

"Your set-down affirmative. Landing fee will be one thousand dollars."

"Isn't that a little stiff, Lomé?"

"Take it or leave it."

"I'll take it," the pilot replied with just the right amount of disgust in his voice. "I can't afford to go back out over water with bad radar."

"Take one pass inland and make your approach from north by northwest to runway One. Lights coming on now."

"Thank you, Lomé, passing over now." *Click*. "Carter?"

"Yeah?"

"Four minutes."

"Right." The Killmaster came out of his seat and motioned the others to join him. "Let's go."

The three of them opened the emergency belly hatch and manhandled the gun crate with its chute in place toward the opening.

"Carter?" came the pilot's voice.

"Yes?"

"There are the flares."

"I've got them."

"I'll get you as directly above them as I can on the pass before throttling down."

"Many thanks."

Carter threw the phones aside and pushed the crate out the hatch just as he heard and felt the powerful engines abate. When it cleared he patted Leila on the helmet.

She rolled forward, tucked, and was gone.

He counted to three and patted Rowland's helmet.

Nothing happened.

"Go, man, go!"

"Oh, shieeeet!" the man cried, and rolled out.

Carter did another short count and did a nosedive. He rolled over twice and flattened out into a free fall. When he was sure both Leila and Rowland were clear beneath him, their bonnets blossomed, he pulled himself.

Well, he thought, *first phase complete*.

All three of them landed softly and safely.

Even Rowland had survived the jump with a lift in spirits. The moment he was on good solid ground he was his old self again, raring to go.

Leila had landed practically on top of the gun crate. She had it open by the time Carter and Rowland got to her.

When everything was on their backs they moved across the open field where Carter hoped he would find Omegla's friendlies.

They were waiting, five of them, just beyond the flares. No one spoke until the red lights were extinguished and they were grouped back around a canvas-covered truck.

All of them had handguns, but there were only two rifles in the group.

With any luck, Carter thought, that should be more than enough until reinforcements reached them at the bank.

"Which one of you is Captain Zagebbe?"

"I am, monsieur," said the youngest and tallest of the

group as he stepped forward. "I came over the frontier last night."

"You know the plan?"

"I do."

"Very well, let's get loaded." He checked his watch. "We have exactly forty-three minutes before the fireworks begin at the docks. I want to be in place in front of the bank by then and ready to fire."

"We will be, monsieur."

They loaded and moved off. As they rolled through the dusty streets in the outskirts of the capital, Carter could hear the birds begin and a few cows lowing for their morning feed and milking.

It was almost dawn.

The inner city, close by the beach, was dark and eerily deserted. They saw only two three-man patrols. Since Zagebbe had managed to steal two uniforms for the driver and his front-seat companion, the truck didn't draw a second look.

"Monsieur Carter."

"Yes?"

"We are entering the street of the bank."

The Killmaster moved to a slit in the side of the canvas top and parted it. "Damn."

"What is it?" Leila whispered, moving up beside him.

"There are two guards outside the bank doors. We'll have to take them out before we blow the door. We still have a few minutes to wait, and if we park, one of them is surely going to come over and investigate."

"I've still got this." She lifted the leg of her coveralls to reveal the Welrod in a leather rig attached to her calf.

"Good," Carter said, attaching Wilhelmina's silencer. "Fire at my command. Captain?"

"*Oui, monsieur?*"

"Tell your driver to slow down and come to a stop right

across from the bank. When those two drop, have your two men in uniform take their places. You back the truck around into position and park it ass end toward the doors for the mortar.''

''Will do,'' Zagebbe replied, moving toward the front of the truck.

''Rowland?''

''Here.''

''Can you use that mortar?''

''Does a bear shit in the woods? I can shoot anything that goes boom.''

''Then get on it.''

The Killmaster checked his watch again. Eight minutes until zero hour. The landing boats would have already hit the beaches above and below the city. The freighter would just be nosing into the docks.

''Almost,'' Leila said, poking the snout of the Welrod through a slit in the canvas.

''Get ready.''

The truck slowed, rocked, and then stopped directly in front of the bank.

''Fire!''

Both guards dropped like stones. Zagebbe's men were out of the truck and dragging the dead men into the darkness practically as they fell. By the time the captain was backing the truck around, his men were in position by the doors.

Carter moved to the back of the truck where Rowland was crouching over the tripod-mounted mortar.

''Sighted in?''

''Yeah. All I need is the word.''

''We have about six minutes.''

They sat, the truck rocking gently as it idled beneath them, the deathly quiet eating away at their nerves.

''Five minutes,'' Carter whispered, as much to himself as the others.

''Nick . . .''

It was Leila from her place at the side of the truck.

"Yeah?"

"A patrol just came around the corner. They are about a block and a half away and coming on. It's probably to change the bank guard."

"Dammit. How many?"

"About fifteen."

"We'll have to go now. Rollo . . . ?"

"Just say when, my man."

"Leila, when he fires, open up on them. You . . ."

"Oui, monsieur?"

"Grab that other AK and help her out. The rest of you follow her lead with your own rifles."

"Oui, monsieur."

The young black grabbed the second AK and moved in beside Leila.

"Everybody ready?"

A chorus of whispered affirmatives came back at him.

"Give her hell, Rollo!"

The mortar bucked and exploded a shell directly in the middle of the double doors.

They became splinters, and all hell erupted from the side of the truck.

"Load up again!" Carter shouted above the din.

"It's done."

"C'mon!"

The two of them jumped into the street. The patrol had been caught completely unawares. So much so that instead of sprinting for cover they had dropped to their knees where they were and started to return the fire.

"Right in the middle."

"You're a bloodthirsty bastard, ain't ya," Rowland cackled.

The mortar roared again and orange flame spurted three feet from the end of the deadly tube.

Bodies, blood, and bits of rifles flew everywhere. Three

escaped the carnage, but they had no more fight left in them. Discarding their guns, they took off in retreat like gazelles.

"In the bank, everyone!"

It was a ragtag force, but they were disciplined. In less than a minute they were all inside the building with Leila covering from beside the truck.

By the time she reached Carter's side, the street outside the bank was deathly quiet again.

"Well," Carter hissed, "they know we're here now."

"How much time?" she asked.

"Four minutes. But the sound of our firing probably started it early. They can easily hear all this from the docks and the beach above the city."

The words had barely left Carter's lips when they heard mortar shells exploding and the steady chatter of machine-gun fire in the distance.

"Okay, the fat's in the fire—let's make sure we don't burn. Captain, get your men at the second- and third-story windows. Rollo, get inside the second door and set up that mortar. Anything moves, blow it to hell!"

"You got it. Sheeeeit, ain't had so much fun since I rode shotgun for a moonshiner when I was a boy."

"Leila, grab those grenades and follow me up to the roof."

Carter grabbed the canvas bag containing the radio, and the two of them headed for the stairs. Four flights up they found the door to the roof and burst through.

Once there, Leila spread out her munitions for a battle line while Carter got the radio operative.

He found the frequency and homed in on it. Then, for the next ten minutes, they listened to a running commentary on the way between command posts.

Both upper and lower beaches had been easily taken. The infantry had gotten off the freighter without any opposition, and by the time they had lost the element of surprise, the half-tracks and the tanks were in the streets doing their jobs.

"What do you think?" Leila asked.

"Sounds good so far. I'll give them another five minutes to make sure everything's secure on their end and then ring them up for some help."

"Look!"

Carter peered over the edge of the roof. About twenty men, armed to the teeth with everything including bazookas, were moving, door to door, toward them. They were coming from both sides of the bank, and from the way they moved, Carter could tell that they were a trained force.

"Good God," he moaned.

"Nick, they're white men!"

"So they are," Carter growled. "Ten to one they are part of Cyclops's private army, probably mercenaries. They're only interested in what is in the vault below. They won't be worried about the rest of the war. Start lobbing grenades!"

She did with accuracy, but Carter knew they wouldn't be able to hold them off from the roof for very long, and the firepower from the bank's windows wouldn't have too much effect stopping them once their heavy guns got going.

His fears became reality as one of the bazooka men fired at the third floor and they lost their first man.

"Try for the ones with the bazookas."

She nodded and Carter returned to the radio.

"Black Dog . . . Black Dog . . . this is Firefly. Can you hear me, Black Dog? Come in . . ."

"This is Black Dog, Firefly. Have you reached your objective?"

"We have, Black Dog, and we are in, but it's iffy how long we can stay in. We have a heavy force pushing the hell out of us. Can you give up a big gun at this time?"

"We have three beachheads solid, and we're moving into the city. Don't worry, Firefly, there's a tank coming your way."

"Many thanks, Black Dog. Hurry him up if you can."

"Will do . . . out."

Carter left the radio on receive, turned up the volume, and turned back toward Leila. He was about to join her when the roof beneath her feet exploded.

The force lifted him and sent him flying backward. It was like a sledgehammer grinding against his chest.

The last thing he heard was the delayed roar of the bazooka that had done the damage.

The last thing he saw was Leila toppling over the edge.

Then there was only blackness.

"You okay?"

Rowland's face was blurred in front of his eyes as the world came back. "Yeah, but . . . ribs, I think . . . Leila?"

"She bought it . . . never knew a thing, even what hit her."

Carter felt an iron fist in the middle of his gut. But that was the name of the game; you take a chance on dying and just never figure you will.

Leila did.

"Did we win the rest of the war?" he growled.

"We did that," Rowland replied. "Tanks have a way of winning wars when the other side doesn't have any."

Carter moved, felt constricted, and looked down. "What the hell is this?"

"Tape. You screwed up some ribs."

"How's the rest of me?"

"You'll live. We've got the charge on the vault door."

"Help me up."

"You sure?"

"I'm sure."

Rowland helped him to his feet and together they moved into the room that fronted the vault.

Omegla was there.

"Sorry about the woman."

Carter only grunted. It was burning his guts, deep inside. But he would keep it there until he had his hands on a name.

"What's the situation?"

"Lomé is secure. There are still a few skirmishes in the north but only fire fights. Two more hours should do it."

"Okay, now I want mine. Let's blow it."

The bomb boys moved them away, and twenty minutes later Carter was sifting through the complete inner workings of Cyclops.

When he found what he wanted he packed it in a briefcase and headed for the airport and INT Four-niner-four-niner.

The pilot was able to patch him through to Casablanca as soon as they were in the air.

"General Mock, this is Carter."

"I have already heard most of it. Congratulations."

"Thanks, but it's not entirely over. And, General . . . ?"

The pause was long as if the old Russian already knew. He did. "Leila?"

"Yes. It was quick, no pain. The way we all want to go."

"I could tell from your voice. It's too bad. I begged her not to follow in my footsteps."

There was something in the man's voice, a tremor that should not have been there had Leila been just an agent. People like Mock didn't get tense over losing agents. It came with the territory and they all expected it.

"She wasn't just another operative, was she, General."

"No, Nicholas, she wasn't. She was my daughter, illegitimate of course, but still my daughter. She was in the game to prove something . . . probably to me."

"Consider it proved. She did one hell of a job."

"You're taking care of the rest of it, I presume."

"I'm on my way now."

"Then it's done, my boy, and we're enemies again . . . it's a pity."

"Isn't it."

"Good luck, as you Americans say."

"Thanks, but this time I'll make my own."

Carter cut the connection.

"Where do we meet the *Noble Savage*?"

"Corsica . . . in about two hours."

"Wake me."

It was two hours before dawn when the *Noble Savage* slackened speed off Cap Ferrat.

In the bow, Carter adjusted the flippers on his feet and shrugged into the webs of the aqualung. Chandra Braxton passed him a sheathed knife and Wilhelmina encased in a watertight oilskin bag. He snapped both of them to the utility belt at his waist.

"You really have to do this?"

"I do," he replied. "You did your job, you got your money. I don't work just for money."

It was almost like a slap in the face, but she ignored it. "If you must, you must, but please try to stay alive. I'm getting a little long in the tooth and this may be my last chance to have a fling with a man like you."

Carter smiled and brushed her cheek with his lips. "Just pull into the bay at Cannes and have a launch waiting at the pier. I'll be there."

He snapped the headband of a facemask around his neck and fitted it into position. Clumsily, facing away from the boat to clear the fins, he descended the ladder. As his feet found the bottom rung, he grasped the mouthpiece, took a long surface dive, and struck out for land.

He swam slowly and on the surface to conserve his energy until he was close in. Then he dove and covered the last five hundred yards underwater.

The beach was deserted: no guards, no dogs. There was no one to oppose him as he cut the fence and entered. Once he had shed his gear, he unpacked shoes, turtleneck, and black trousers from the waterproof pack he had carried in on his back and dressed.

He headed up, through the gardens, to the villa. Soft music came from somewhere inside, and the whole villa was ablaze with light.

He didn't know exactly what he expected to find, but he

was ready for anything, Luger in hand, as he stepped through the tall French windows into the villa's great room.

She was there, sitting in a large chair by the fireplace, a pretty blond-haired child-woman. She was dressed in a fluffy white sweater, and her left arm was in a sling, wrapped tightly to her body.

In front of her on a large coffee table documents were stacked in neat piles.

"I knew you'd come. I've been waiting every night, expecting you."

"You were the woman on the roof."

"Yes."

God, he thought, *she looks like a kid*.

But he didn't move the muzzle of his Luger away from her chest. Kid or not, he knew she was deadly.

"Are you going to kill me?" she asked with hardly any inflection in her voice.

"I'll let you know. Where's Marcus Cologne?"

"Upstairs, in his bed." Carter backed toward the stairs. "Second door on the right."

Cologne was lying peacefully on his back, a neat hole in the middle of his forehead.

Carter went back to the great room and fixed himself a drink, keeping Wilhelmina close to his right hand.

"You?"

She nodded. "After we heard about Lomé and the success of the counterrevolution, he wanted me to go after you again. I couldn't . . . I refused."

"Why?"

She smiled. "Because I knew I would lose. I could feel it, sense it."

"So you killed him and waited. Why? A bargaining chip?"

"Yes, plus all this." She gestured toward the documents. "What you don't already know about Cyclops is here. I figure that's a good trade for my freedom . . . and my life."

"Who are you?"

"Names are not important. Mine happens to be Marga Lund, but I will change it after tonight."

"If I don't kill you."

"If you don't kill me."

"Romar de Armon was yours, wasn't he?"

"Yes."

"And Bob Sievers and that old tobacco store owner?"

She shrugged. "It's the business. You should know that."

"Yeah, I do."

He fired twice, but the first slug was enough. It pinned her to the back of the chair with her mouth and her eyes wide with shock.

In minutes he had packed the documents in a garbage bag from behind the bar.

Just before leaving he loosened the sling on her arm.

A Beretta fell to the floor.

"Like you said, little girl, just business."

Her face, in death, lost that little-girl innocence and seemed to take on the cruelty that Carter knew inhabited her lost soul.

Dawn was almost breaking as he left the villa and walked around the headland and toward the harbor of Cannes.

It looked like it was going to be a beautiful day, a great day to start a long, slow cruise with a tall, rich, and gracious lady.

DON'T MISS THE NEXT NEW
NICK CARTER SPY THRILLER

TUNNEL FOR TRAITORS

They had placed him in a windowless attic room, with only one locked door. The furniture was sparse: a heavy old bed, a dresser, and one chair.

How long had it been? Twenty-four hours?

At least.

Twice, they had come into the room: the first time with a tray of cold food; the second to lead him down the hall to a bathroom.

Perhaps the gamble had been too big. Maybe Poulson *didn't* know how to contact Copperhead. Maybe there was a prearranged contact time, and Copperhead himself did all the contacting.

Carter stretched out on the bed and wished for a cigarette. They had taken his lighter along with the weapons.

Suddenly he felt it.

Carter came instantly to his feet when the pulser in the hollow heel of his right shoe began to throb against his heel.

He pushed the heel to the side and flipped a tiny switch.

Immediately the throbbing stopped and the Killmaster knew that the red light in front of Marty Jacobs now glowed steadily. It would tell Jacobs that he, Carter, had gotten the go-ahead.

He took the thin strip of plastique from his left heel and carefully worked it around the door and into the crack by the lock. Once this was done, he produced a tiny detonator from the hollow heel and then closed it for the last time.

The detonator was no bigger than a safety pin, and shaped like one. Before setting it, he rolled the bed onto its side and planted all of the furniture against it.

This done, he went back to the door. He unhinged the pin, shoved it into the plastique, and hurried to the safety of his nest behind the bed and mattress.

It was a fifteen-second timer, activated eventually by the melting of the outer plastic core over the fuse to release the chemical.

Slowly, Carter counted. At thirteen, he put his head between his knees and his hands over his ears.

The explosion was deafening. It jammed the dresser against the mattress and the mattress over Carter.

It took him only a few seconds to squirrel himself around and get his feet against the bed. With his back to the wall, he pushed until he could see light above one corner of the bed, then pushed harder until the opening was large enough to squeeze through.

The light he saw was moonlight.

Besides the door and a good section of the wall, the plastique had taken out a corner of the roof.

The furniture was kindling. Carter picked up one of the chair legs and darted into the hall. He could hear footsteps pounding up the stairs. He paused.

Only one man.

The stairs turned sharply into the hallway. Other than the moonlight flooding through the roof and what was left of the wall, there was no illumination.

Carter turned his back to the stairs and flattened his side to the wall, with the chair leg an extension of his arms.

When he heard the man's panting wheeze just behind his right shoulder, he swung with all he had in a one-eighty arc.

The chair leg splintered, but so did the face.

The Killmaster caught him before he fell down the stairs, then he threw him to the floor of the hall.

A quick frisk produced a Walther P-1 with a full magazine and one in the chamber. Carter clicked off the safety and headed down the stairs.

Just as he hit the bottom step he heard an ear-shattering explosion in front of the house. Jacobs's boys had done their job. The gate was blown.

Carter bolted down the hall. He was on the third floor. Somehow he had to get down two flights of stairs and toward the front of the house, and he had to do it fast.

He made the second floor and was halfway around the stairwell to the next flight, when a door opened three feet in front of him and a man stepped out.

There was no time to stop. They collided, and both went down, Carter in the center of the hall, the man behind a small table. The Walther slipped from Carter's hand and skidded across the floor. Before he could dive for it, the other man had come to one knee and pulled a switchblade from his belt. The click of the opening blade came simultaneously with the arc of the man's arm.

Carter rolled and felt the hissing whisper of air as the blade flicked past his head. There was a thud, and the point chipped plaster from the opposite wall. The goon tried to push the table from in front of him and retrieve the knife.

The Killmaster himself lunged forward. He slammed the heels of both hands violently against the table edge and drove the flimsy top into the man's belly. When the upper torso and head flopped forward, Carter chopped the heels of both hands over the man's ears.

He screamed, and went down and out like a ruptured balloon.

Suddenly the hallway exploded. At the same time, the man's falling body shoved the table forward into Carter, spinning him away. As the Killmaster rolled around, he saw that the action had saved his life. From another door, a second of Poulson's henchmen had appeared. The Walther had barked twice. One slug had slammed into the wall in a direct line where Carter had been. The other had plowed into the skull of the already dead man.

The shooter was bringing the Walther around for another try when Carter lurched to his knees and drove his shoulder against the table and into the man's side. He heard rather than saw the man's gun fall to the floor.

Carter upended the table and used his shoulder again to slam the man behind it into the wall. When the table slid down, the man was squirming upward like a crippled snake.

Deftly, he yanked his cohort's knife from the wall and came at Carter.

But he was too late. The Killmaster flipped the table around, brought it high above his head, and smashed it into splinters over the man's head.

Panting heavily, he stood over the dead man, trying to focus his eyes on one of the fallen guns as the shredded piece of furniture dropped to the floor. He spotted the guns at last, filled his hands with both of them, and sprinted down the stairs.

Near the bottom he could see the lead car and Jacobs's van thundering up the cobbled drive. Out of the corners of both eyes he could see shooters coming around both sides of the house. They fired, and the fire was returned from the moving vehicles.

In a great room to his right, he saw Poulson and one of the big gorillas who had carried him to the attic room the night before.

Their eyes met at the same time.

The machine pistol in Poulson's hand sprayed the entry-way in front of Carter, blocking his path. He guided the Walther in his left hand around the archway and emptied the clip into the room. There was a loud scream that turned into a gurgling death rattle, and then the dull thud of a body hitting the floor.

The lead car was around the arc of the drive now and heading back toward the gate. Abruptly it skidded to a halt, and two of Jacobs's men rolled from the sedan's rear doors to the first position in the grass. They had barely hit ground when the machine pistols in their hands started barking toward the sides of the house.

The van itself was twenty yards short of the arc, and Carter knew it couldn't stop. He had to get by Poulson.

"Franz Poulson?"

"*Ja*, you son of a bitch!"

"Let's make a deal. Call your hounds off."

"No deal!"

"Why not?"

"Because if you don't kill me, he will."

"You mean Copperhead? Do you know who he is, Poulson?"

"I told you—no, I don't. No deals. I'm going to kill you, you son of a bitch."

The last word was barely out of his mouth when, again, the hall and the other side of the wall above Carter's head splintered with slugs.

"Poulson!" Carter shouted. "I want to talk. Here's my gun. I'm going to step into the doorway. Let's talk."

Carter reached his arm around the doorway and flipped the empty Walther into the room.

"All right?"

"All right," Poulson growled in reply. "Let me see you."

Carter knew he had only seconds after showing his vulnerable body in the middle of the hallway. He had already jacked a shell into the chamber of the Walther in his right hand. He held it at his hip, then lifted his left hand high above his head.

"Coming now," he said. "Don't fire."

"Come ahead," Poulson said.

Carter took a deep breath, and then two steps into the hallway. He turned to see Poulson crouched over the other man's body, the machine pistol lifted in front of his face with both hands. The side of his head was a bloody mess, and his blond hair was matted with a combination of blood and sweat. Evidently, one of Carter's random shots had almost gotten him.

Carter moved forward. He could see the man's fingers, hands, and forearms tensing on the machine pistol. He readied his own Walther at his side.

"You're dead, bastard," Poulson said, his heavy jaw splitting in a leering grin.

"Am I?" Carter replied.

He brought the Walther up from his hip, firing as fast as he could squeeze off the shots. The first one hit the gorilla's body. The second, third, fourth, and fifth stitched up Poulson's frame. The sixth caught him square in the middle of the face and spread his brains over the wall behind him.

Carter dropped the Walther and quickly frisked the body, just in case the man might have something of value on him.

Nothing.

Outside, the war was still going on, but diminishing. The van was parked directly in front of the door, with its back open. A machine pistol barked from the dark opening, keeping the shooters at the left of the house occupied. The two agents near the sedan were holding the others down at the right side of the house.

Carter sprinted to the double front doors and flung them both open. "Marty!" he screamed into the night.

The man's face appeared at the side window of the van. "Here! Run for it!"

At the same time, the door opened and Jacobs's words brought a new round of gunfire from his people.

Carter dropped into a crouch and did a running duck walk to the rear of the van. Five feet short, he dived. His chest hit the side of the seat, and Jacobs's hand gripping his belt dragged him the rest of the way inside.

"Go!" Jacobs cried.

> —From TUNNEL FOR TRAITORS
> A New Nick Carter Spy Thriller
> From Charter in June 1986

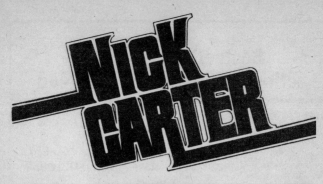

Bestselling Thrillers— action-packed for a great read